That night, when she slipped between the sheets, she knew Hamish had slept in the bed while she was gone.

The sheets were clean and everything was in order, but there was something.... Just something. A faint scent of him from the blankets, maybe, or just the feeling that his large body had lain there last night and the nights before that.

She lay awake a long time with unwanted thoughts. Someday, Hamish would lie in this bed with his wife—another woman—and Brenda Jane Dolliver would be out of his life, only a memory.

She simply wasn't wife material. Just as well. Even if she wanted to marry him, he wouldn't have her....

Dear Reader,

The holiday season is a time for family, love...and miracles! We have all this—and more!—for you this month in Silhouette Romance. So in the gift-giving spirit, we offer *you* these wonderful books by some of the genre's finest:

A workaholic executive finds a baby in his in-box and enlists the help of the sexy single mom next door in this month's BUNDLES OF JOY, *The Baby Came C.O.D.*, by RITA Award-winner Marie Ferrarella. *Both* hero and heroine are twins, and Marie tells their identical siblings' stories in *Desperately Seeking Twin*, out this month in our Yours Truly line.

Favorite author Elizabeth August continues our MEN! promotion with *Paternal Instincts*. This latest installment in her SMYTHESHIRE, MASSACHUSETTS series features an irresistible lone wolf turned doting dad! As a special treat, Carolyn Zane's sizzling family drama, THE BRUBAKER BRIDES, continues with *His Brother's Intended Bride*—the title says it all!

Completing the month are *three* classic holiday romances. A world-weary hunk becomes *The Dad Who Saved Christmas* in this magical tale by Karen Rose Smith. Discover *The Drifter's Gift* in RITA Award-winning author Lauryn Chandler's emotional story. Finally, debut author Zena Valentine weaves a tale of transformation—and miracles—in *From Humbug to Holiday Bride*.

So treat yourself this month—and every month!—to Silhouette Romance!

Happy holidays,

Joan Marlow Golan
Senior Editor

Please address questions and book requests to:
Silhouette Reader Service
U.S.: 3010 Walden Ave., P.O. Box 1325, Buffalo, NY 14269
Canadian: P.O. Box 609, Fort Erie, Ont. L2A 5X3

FROM HUMBUG TO *H*OLIDAY BRIDE

Zena Valentine

Silhouette
ROMANCE™
Published by Silhouette Books
America's Publisher of Contemporary Romance

For Mom and Aunt Vi. Thanks.

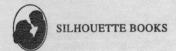 SILHOUETTE BOOKS

ISBN 0-373-19269-X

FROM HUMBUG TO HOLIDAY BRIDE

Printed in U.S.A.

ZENA VALENTINE

has had a career goal since childhood to "have adventures." Throughout her adventures in journalism, cosmetics, construction, parenting, corporate financial relations, photography, sports car racing, gardening, flying, cooking and real estate, she has carried a lifelong love of writing. She likens writing a romance novel to restarting an airplane at five thousand feet ("exciting"). Nowadays she divides her time between the north woods of Minnesota and the desert country of Nevada. Her journalist daughter and musician son are off having their own adventures.

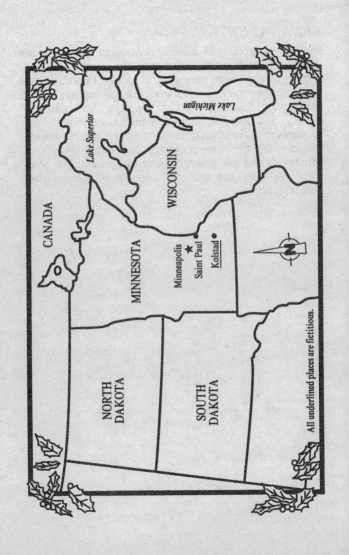

CANADA

Lake Superior

Lake Michigan

MINNESOTA

WISCONSIN

Minneapolis
★
Saint Paul
Kolstad ●

NORTH
DAKOTA

SOUTH
DAKOTA

N

All underlined places are fictitious.

Chapter One

Hamish Chandler had never felt quite so helpless. Or useless.

The young woman lay on the cranked-up hospital bed, its top slightly elevated, her dark hair matted, her tanned skin contrasting sharply with the shades and textures of white that engulfed her. "She is, uh, was, a photojournalist," Mrs. Billings had said. "She rides horses, plays golf and tennis very well. And she skis." And then Mrs. Billings had blushed slightly and added, "I think she breaks a lot of hearts, too, that girl."

He couldn't see that the young woman before him was anything like a heartbreaker, not with the bruises and scratch marks covering half of her face. She wasn't skinny, probably because of her athletic ability. Even after three weeks in a hospital bed, there was substance to what he could see of her.

She was sleeping, and he felt a voyeuristic awkwardness in staring at her, yet he was unwilling to awaken her. The shape she was in, he thought, sleep must be a blessed escape.

"Please, please, see what you can do," Mrs. Billings had pleaded with glistening eyes the day before. "I don't think she's much for religion, but maybe, after coming so close to dying, maybe…"

He could see the young woman had probably come close to dying if she was still in bad shape after three weeks of recovery. She lay so motionless, her limbs slack, her graceful, long-fingered hand resting palm up with her fingers curled on the pillow next to her head. He sank into the chair alongside the bed, filled with an odd longing to comfort her and take away the pain.

Visiting patients in the hospital was a regular part of his job, and he liked it because for the most part the people he visited seemed so pleased that he was there. Visiting *her*, however, had little to do with his job. He had come because Mrs. Billings had been so emotional. And insistent. "How do you know her?" he had asked his graying housekeeper. Over the years, Mrs. B had become more than a housekeeper. She had seen him through crises, sadness and death, and now she helped raise his daughters. She'd told him that B. J. Dolliver, the woman lying wounded in the hospital bed, had been a college classmate of her niece, Deborah.

"I knew all about her, even if I only saw her a few times when Deb brought her home for holidays. I feel, though, as if I know her well," she'd added sadly. "It's been easy to keep track of her since she left college."

B. J. Dolliver, it seemed from tabloid reports, had at age twenty-seven collected nearly as many photographic awards as she had men. "She was really something," Mrs. B had said. "When she was with us during vacations, Deb said there was never a dull moment with B.J. around."

Their former close friendship, however, had not been enough for Deb to gain entry to B.J.'s room to offer comfort.

"Deborah's a nurse and works in the hospital," Mrs. B had said, "but B.J. won't see anyone. Not even her own family. Her mother is dead, but her father lives on the West Coast. Deb thinks B.J. hasn't told him." Mrs. B's eyes had been narrowed with concern. "Deb thinks because B.J.'s face was badly damaged, she doesn't want anyone to see her. Deb could have just walked into her room anyway, but knowing B.J., she decided to respect her privacy."

Mrs. B had described B. J. Dolliver's brush with death after she drove her German sports car over a cliff, and the injuries that her orthopedic surgeon said would prevent her from ever walking again under her own power. "She's spittin' mad. Deb said the nurses don't like to be near her."

"I shouldn't wonder," Hamish had concurred, then finally asked, "Exactly why do you want me to see her?"

There was a searching hesitation before Mrs. Billings had answered on a long, drawn-out breath. "Because when she finds out she's never going to walk again, she'll just go out and finish the job. Deb says B. J. Dolliver can't *live* without the full use of her body." She expelled the words as though the sentence would die unfinished if she stopped to breathe. Her last few words came out choked. "Frankly, I've always had a soft spot for B.J. She seemed to be so, well, so...alone."

B. J. Dolliver's parents divorced when she was a small child, and her mother died shortly afterward, Mrs. B had explained. B.J. was raised by her father, Patrick Dolliver, the owner of a country-wide, sports equipment franchise.

"She spent her young life trying to prove to that man that she's as good as any of his jock heroes," Mrs. B had scoffed. "And a lot he ever cared...."

So the Reverend Hamish Chandler, pastor of Trinity Union Church in Kolstad, Minnesota, familiarly known as simply the Kolstad Church, let his concentration fall once again to the woman lying on the bed. He wondered why this particular assignment had been put in his path, especially now, especially today, when the second anniversary of his beloved wife's death had just passed.

He sat in uncomfortable silence, unable to look away from the battered body of the sleeping woman.

"Spinal injuries," Mrs. Billings had said, obviously quoting from Deborah, the nurse. "Pelvis broken into pieces, too many to put 'em all back together. Broken right shoulder, smashed right arm, facial lacerations."

He saw the lacerations, the tiny scar on her cheek, the healing scrapes on her neck. Then he looked at her left arm, the good one resting above the covers with the fingers curled over her palm. He saw where stitches had been removed and where myriad small cuts had been left to mend without stitches.

His gaze roamed to the clear collapsing sack attached to the back of her right wrist, and the small trapeze suspended a foot above her chest. As a photojournalist, she had naturally been a physically active young woman with two strong legs and arms and the agility to climb and jump carrying the equipment of her profession. It was nearly impossible to envision her as Mrs. B had described, running and confident, capturing the world and its people through her lens.

He clasped his hands together between his spread knees and felt sadness overwhelm him for a vibrant life nearly destroyed. Nearly. But not completely, for she still lived, and was recovering.

He had seen worse, of course, during his violent life as a teen. Much worse. Before he was fifteen, he had come to accept that people were wounded, maimed and killed during the course of the fight for survival. Thank God that life was in the dark past, forever behind him.

What would he say to her? What was there to say? He didn't have a clue what he was meant to do here, and yet he'd been sent, so there must be a purpose.

A flash of pink caught his eye and he turned to see a nurse slip quietly through the door, a pale pink sweater draped over her shoulders. She smiled at him and lifted the woman's limp left wrist to take a pulse.

Her patient's eyes suddenly flew open, staring in fear and confusion. Her body twitched once, and then again more violently, and Hamish heard a soft "No!" escape her lips before her eyes pinched shut in a harsh grimace. Her body arched, and she quivered in the grip of a suffering he could not fathom.

He saw the nurse's hand rest gently on the patient's abdomen, and she whispered something, while her other hand gestured in jerking movements for him to leave the room. He slipped out the door just as the woman's groan broke into an eerie deep-throated howl that sent needles up his back. It was a lament of pain so deep he felt it had been wrenched from her very soul, and he found himself leaning helplessly against the wall outside her room until it subsided into soft gasps and moans.

The nurse rushed past him a few moments later. "Spasm," she muttered.

Hamish stepped back into the room and moved to the side of her bed where she lay, face beaded with sweat, eyes glistening, her breathing ragged. "What can I do?" he asked.

"Go away," she rasped, her voice hoarse and whispery. She closed her eyes to reject him, and he saw that she was forcing herself to breathe deeply and slowly. He saw the pulse in her neck slamming rapidly under her skin.

He took the wet washcloth from the stand alongside her pillow and held it under hot water from the goosenecked faucet. Then he squeezed it out and laid it across her forehead. He felt rather than heard her sharp intake of breath when the cloth touched her skin. He felt her relax a little, then he used the warm, wet cloth to daub at her face.

"You new here?" she asked in the same hoarse whisper, her dazed hazel-green eyes fixing on him with an effort.

"Sort of," he replied, giving her a weak grin.

"Lay it over my face. It feels good," she whispered.

He did, as gently as he could. After a few seconds, the pulse in her neck began to slow, and her left hand came up and took the washcloth away. She flopped her hand backward and let the cloth drop so that Hamish had to jump to catch it before it hit the floor.

"Where's your uniform?" she rasped.

He grinned, then watched her raise her left hand and fumble to reach the little trapeze overhead. "I'm not a doctor," he said before reaching up to adjust the apparatus lower so she could reach it.

"Then go away," she ordered, and turned her head away.

But when he looked down moments later, she was staring at him with barely suppressed rage and wariness. He looked away from her face. Why shouldn't she be wary, lying helpless for three weeks flat on her back and knowing nothing would ever be the same? And he was a stranger to her.

"My name is Hamish Chandler. Deborah Billings's aunt asked me to see you," he said as he made a final adjustment to the trapeze. "Is that better?" He gave the apparatus a yank.

She frowned at him, then raised her left hand and gripped the bar. Her lips turned up at the corners, more of a sneer than a smile, but the change was encouraging nonetheless. She was a fighter all right, Hamish thought.

"You ought to be one," she whispered.

He dug his hands into his pockets. "One what?"

"Doctor."

"Yes, I appreciate your keen observation. It took a great deal of skill to do that properly."

She didn't acknowledge his attempt at humor. "And the cloth. Do it again," she rasped.

He swished the cloth under the hot water and twisted out the excess moisture. This time he placed it in her left hand, and she flopped it over her face, slowly patting it over her features in circular motions, avoiding the small jagged scar on the right side. After it had cooled, she once again flopped it over the edge of the bed for him to catch if he could. He interrupted its fall and laid it on the stand close to her pillow. "More?" he asked.

"Got a mirror?" she asked, still whispering.

"Afraid not."

"Look around. In the drawers over there."

"Why?"

"Just do it."

"Why?"

"Damn you." She pressed her eyes closed for a few seconds. When she opened them again, they were blazing with frustration. "I want to see."

"Why?"

"Why do you think?" she whispered.

"You've been here three weeks, and I gather they haven't let you see yourself. I don't have the authority to countermand those orders, Miss Dolliver."

She grimaced. "Who in the hell are you anyway? If Deborah sent you, you're supposed to be cheering me up." The words were spat with all the force it took her to get them out. Then she reached again for the bar above her, gripped it, then let it go.

"Deborah didn't send me," he said. "Her aunt asked me to stop by and see you." He wondered whether he should explain who he was. He decided to go with full disclosure. "I'm pastor of the Kolstad Church."

She muttered an expletive that he ignored. "I suppose you're going to pray over me," she jeered.

"I suppose I will."

She reached for the bar again and gripped it until her knuckles were white, then released it, lowering her hand to her side. Her eyes were as hard as cold iron, but he saw something else barely detectable lurking there. It was fear.

She swallowed hard and winced. "So, why did Deborah's aunt send you? If she did." Her skepticism was as heavily evident as the dripping sarcasm. She closed her lids momentarily, then lifted them half-mast. "I remember Deb's aunt," she whispered affectionately.

"She's my housekeeper, and she's quite fond of you. Apparently, your friendship with her niece was significant to them both when you were in college."

"Deb works here. She could visit anytime. But she's a friend. She respects my privacy," she whispered pointedly. "I don't want visitors."

He paused, letting the hospital noises from the hallway fill the space. "I know," he said finally.

She glared at him. But he saw her struggling to be fierce, and he sensed something softer behind it all. She seemed hardly able to hold her eyes open.

"No visitors," she rasped again. "Deborah knows that."

"They care about you," he said.

"Oh, damn," she cursed softly, her eyes closing in a grimace.

He thought for a moment it was another spasm coming on and was about to bolt for the nurses' desk. Then he realized she was distressed by something else. Once again he found himself the object of those eyes the color of fall grass.

"Why you?" she demanded.

He frowned, wondering why she was upset. What was she reading into his visit? While he wondered, she came to her own worst conclusion.

"What are they trying to tell me, sending a minister? Am I going to die? After all this, am I dying anyway?" He was struck by her bitterness.

"Of course not," he said. "You're getting better." He wondered suddenly how the conversation had become so complex. "I think your doctor would have told you about your condition."

"He says I'm...oh, what he really meant was I'm...crippled!" Hamish could barely hear the last word. He felt her horror and leaned forward to take her left hand in his. It was small and soft, cool and clammy.

"I don't know your official prognosis," he said as gently as he could, watching a large tear slowly squeeze out from under long, dark lashes and make its way toward her ear. "Please don't read more into my visit than is intended."

"Then why are you here?" she demanded.

He rubbed her small hand in his large one and looked at the many small cuts and scratches that were now healing. She didn't pull her hand away, and he was strangely pleased by that, as if he needed the comfort of holding her hand as much as she might need his comfort in doing so.

"Ah, dear lady," he said. "I'm not sure. Yet."

He watched her lids fly open, sharp curiosity in her gaze. She was studying his face, her lips twitching with words she apparently wanted to say but was holding back.

"I know it sounds crazy," he said. "But I'm not even sure why I'm here except that I was touched by Mrs. Billings's concern for you."

"Touched," she scoffed. "Yeah, sure. Touched."

She let him keep her hand, and the action took the sting

out of her words, as if her mouth had spoken and the rest of her denied what it had said.

Hamish identified with the bitterness and sarcasm he heard. It had been many years, but he remembered when he had greeted every stranger with contempt and mistrust, ready to fight against any real or imagined threat to his survival. That was life on the streets, every man for himself, trusting no one. Ever. Remembering how it had been then, he inhaled deeply and smiled a sad smile.

What, he wondered, could have brought her to such bitterness when she had so much in her life—luxury, adventure, success? Her bone-chilling resentment was coming from some place deeper than he could see.

"Are you here to convince me my recovery is hopeless?" she demanded in a hoarse whisper.

"No, I haven't heard your medical prognosis," he said again.

"Yeah, sure," she said, and pulled her hand away, reaching once again for the bar above her. He found it distracting the way she kept playing with the bar, gripping it, letting it go. But then, it was her only exercise as far as he could see. Nothing else moved. Only her left arm and hand. Her body twitched slightly. She paled and whispered, "Oh, God," then quickly inhaled slow, deep breaths.

The nurse in the pink sweater slipped quietly into the room and lost no time in giving B.J. an injection in her left arm. "There," she said, pulling down the wrinkled cotton sleeve that draped to B.J.'s elbow. "Hopefully that will keep those nasty spasms away. Just in the nick of time, too, I see." She looked up at Hamish and smiled. "Are you a relative?"

Now that was a good question, he thought, and he struggled with an answer. "Friend" sounded false and patronizing, and "acquaintance" was too contrived. So he said simply, "I'm a pastor," even though he was in a way pulling rank. He knew they hardly ever evicted pastors, even at the request of patients.

B.J. said nothing, but hardly seemed aware of him as she drew in an unsteady breath. Then she gripped his right hand and held it against her chest where he could feel the fast thumping of her heart and the stark tension in her body despite her recent dosage of medication. Her clasp was surprisingly strong, but clearly she was desperate and in acute emotional distress.

He waited a few minutes while the medication took effect. He studied the delicate bone structure of her stubborn chin and felt a twitch in his chest.

She opened her eyes. "He's wrong," she whispered finally. "I'm going to do it. I'm going to walk. And I'm going to run. I'll show them they're wrong."

She was a fighter, and he was deeply grateful that she hadn't wanted to give up and die as her friend Deborah feared, but was determined to make herself whole again. Maybe she could do it. Maybe she could make a liar out of her physician. He willed with all his heart and spirit that she was right.

He felt her frustration and her anger. And her defiance.

He also felt the softness of her breasts beneath the back of his hand as she clutched it hard against her. It was an unconscious gesture on her part, he knew, a matter of hanging on to whatever support was available, of gleaning strength and some tiny measure of comfort from the only source offered.

Still, it had been a long time since he'd felt the softness of a woman's body, and for a fleeting moment Hamish was aware that he missed the intimacy, and he thought perhaps it *was* time to open himself to the possibility of finding another wife. In recent months, there had certainly been enough hints from his friends in the congregation that he should be thinking of remarriage.

He would only marry for love, though, in spite of his circumstances, and he dreaded the thought of all the rituals and uncertainties involved in meeting and dating. He still couldn't imagine being married to anyone but Maralynn, although she had been dead for two years now, and their daughters seemed barely to remember her.

His attention was stirred by the woman on the bed when she released his hand, and reached up to grip the bar. He thought that she was going to try to pull herself up as muscles flexed in her arm, but she abruptly lowered her hand again.

"You can go now," she announced in her husky whisper, looking up at the ceiling.

"I thought you'd say that," Hamish replied, letting his elbows rest on his thighs so his hands hung between his knees.

"Your job is done here."

"You think so?" he asked mildly.

She studied him with eyes narrowed in wariness. "Definitely."

He couldn't leave. Nor could he explain the curious compulsion to linger where he wasn't welcome. "I think I'll stay awhile."

"I don't want visitors."

"I know."

Not only wasn't he inclined to leave, but he actually felt comfortable sitting with this intriguing shrew of a woman.

"I'll have you removed," she said.

"Go ahead."

But she didn't.

"I don't know you." She was frowning now, her eyelids heavy with fatigue.

"That's changing, though, isn't it? Even as unpleasant as you are," he quipped.

"Rude, Preacher. The word is rude," she corrected, still studying him. "Doesn't seem to work on you, does it?"

"Oh, I wouldn't say that," he replied, grinning. "If you want me to be impressed that life has been unfair to you, I am. If you want me to pray for your recovery, well, know that I will. If you want to be sure that I know how bitter you are, then rest assured you have persuaded me easily enough."

She shook her head slightly and almost returned his grin. "You sure you're a holy man?"

"I don't think of myself as a holy man and I don't recall the term in my job description," he said. "I'm just a man who happens to be employed as a pastor."

"Where's your collar?"

"In our church, a pastor isn't required to wear a collar except during services," he explained. "They all know who I am, that I serve them, that they hired me and can fire me. There are some in my congregation, in fact, who think I should be replaced."

She was quiet for several seconds, then asked, "Why?"

"I'm a bargain turned sour," he said lightly. He certainly hadn't intended to talk about himself, but he saw that she was interested and thought maybe it wouldn't hurt to draw attention away from herself for a while.

"What does that mean?" she asked.

"They hired my wife and me as a team. Two for the price of one, so to speak. Then we had two children, Emma and Annie, and Maralynn wasn't able to spend as much time as she originally did on church matters. Soon after, she became ill with a serious heart condition, and we required a housekeeper to help out at an additional expense. Maralynn died two years ago, and now there is only one of us to serve the congregation." He smiled to encourage the skepticism on her face. "Most of the congregation accepts the circumstances and seems inclined to let things ride, so, you see, I'm not in imminent danger of being discharged."

"Sorry about your wife," she said. "But you're pulling my leg about the rest."

He laughed without mirth at her directness. "It's a business proposition, hiring a pastor," he resumed. "They hired me under advantageous circumstances that are no longer advantageous for them. Why shouldn't they be concerned that they're paying for more than they're getting? They would have a better bargain by replacing me with a married couple."

"What would you do if that happens?"

"Find another position most likely," he replied.

"Is that difficult?"

"I don't know. This is my first position as pastor and I've had it for six years. I have no idea what the job market is like."

"Why aren't you investigating it? You should prepare for your future." Her whispery voice was fading.

"If it comes to that, then I will," he said, shrugging. It wasn't that he wanted to downplay Maralynn's tragic death or the vague element of truth in his declaration about his job security. Both were serious issues that affected his and his family's lives. Still, he had learned to live without Maralynn, and he knew most people in his congregation appreciated him. Hadn't the board hired him a part-time assistant when Annie was born? And hadn't they elected to keep Medford Bantz on staff? He could afford to shrug off her concern, although, oddly, it touched him.

"You have one other option," she said.

"Oh?"

"Get another wife."

"Marry again? Funny...I've been thinking along those same lines."

"Well, that should be easy for you...what's your name again?"

Hamish had to remind himself that humility was a virtue. "Hamish Chandler," he replied.

"Hmm, that's no name for a pastor." While he tried to think of how to reply, she continued. "You're a regular guy, Hamish. You're the first regular-guy holy man I ever met," she said, her eyes flickering with what he recognized as fatigue. "But don't come back, okay? I don't want any visitors," she added, barely audible, her eyes closed. "And I don't tolerate praying."

Before he realized what he was doing, he had clasped his big hand over her small one and squeezed. "We'll see," he said. "Maybe I won't be able to stay away. I've always enjoyed a good time."

He left his card with his home phone number written in pen and only later asked himself why. Obviously, she would simply discard it.

Hamish was barely out of the car when his two girls came flying across the lawn and threw themselves against him, six-year-old Emma hitting him first because she was older and had longer legs, three-year-old Annie close behind, both of them pressing their faces to his middle and holding on with small arms and dirty hands.

Emma was the first to pull away, her brown hair a wind-blown frizz of tangles, her thin, delicate face sweetly marred by smudges, her deep brown eyes wide with excitement. "We caught a frog and we're keeping him," she declared. He laughed at the importance of her announcement, for she had been trying all summer to gather the courage to pick one up and bring it to the punctured coffee tin that waited on the back porch.

"I fell off the swing," Annie said, her straight strawberry blond hair framing a round face and dimpled cheeks, her blue eyes demure and shy, too big for her face, but balanced by a wide mouth. Already she was on her way to becoming a beauty.

"Did it hurt?" he asked.

She nodded in serious warning, then asked, "Where were you?"

"I went to visit a lady in the hospital."

"Is she going to die?" Emma asked.

"No, she's getting better, but she's been badly injured and she may never be able to walk again," he told them.

Emma's eyes were wide. "Will she have to stay in bed forever?"

"No," he said, grinning. "She'll have a chair with wheels and she can probably walk with crutches. Do you know what crutches are?"

"Jimmy Crowton had crutches. He's in second grade," Emma said.

He picked them up, one in each arm, and walked to the house. Annie reached down to open the door, and then he set them down in the big old back porch enclosed by windows, and they walked into the large, square farm kitchen where Mrs. Billings was cooking dinner.

He liked the smell of roasting meat and the slight tang of gas from the old range. He overlooked the worn vinyl on the floor and the chips in the porcelain of the stove, just as he ignored the rusty patterns stained into the bottom of the wall-hung sink and the dulled old faucets that leaked in spite of his efforts to replace worn gaskets and ancient stems.

The kitchen was immaculate and it was home, and he was lucky to have it. And Mrs. Billings, who had happily made herself part of his family after her husband died four years ago. "How did it go?" she asked him, and he raised his eyebrows in mock exasperation, wondering how much she actually knew about B. J. Dolliver's harsh, combative personality.

"I wasn't welcome," he said.

Mrs. B pursed her lips and folded her arms defiantly over her ample middle as if he had just threatened one of her own. "Will she be all right?"

"Possibly," he replied, washing his hands in the sink. "She won't be able to walk, though."

"Not ever?" Mrs. Billings blanched and dropped her pot holder on the floor.

"Not ever," he said as he retrieved the pot holder.

"Oh, dear. Oh, dear." Her eyes watered, and she patted them with her apron as she sank onto a kitchen chair. He watched her closely, surprised at the extent of her grief over someone she had never known well and hadn't seen for several years. "She's such a lovely young woman, and so very kind. I've admired her so very much. Such a tragedy, isn't it? Such a terrible tragedy."

"Yes, it is," he murmured, putting a hand on her shoulder, astonished that he should be offering her comfort because of the Dolliver woman who was hard as nails and angry as a cornered bobcat.

She made a quick swipe over her wrinkled cheeks.

"It seems as if you and I are talking about two different people," he mused.

"Well, I know she can be very tough and outspoken. After all, she had a very bad childhood," she snapped, then softened again. "No mother. A father who wanted a son and never had time for her." Mrs. Billings patted her eyes again. "I remember enjoying how spunky she was, and I wanted my own niece to be like that. You know, able to take care of herself and give back as good as she got. B. J. Dolliver is a heroine for a lot of young women, Pastor, in spite of growing up unwanted. I don't know whatever she'll do with herself now. What a terrible tragedy. What a terrible thing to happen.''

"Why are you crying, Mrs. Billings?" Emma questioned, her eyes filled with concern.

"The lady I visited today," Hamish explained. "Mrs. Billings knows her and is sad."

Emma turned to the housekeeper. "But Daddy said she's going to get well," she assured Mrs. Billings, patting her on the knee. "She's going to have crutches to help her walk around."

"Yes," Mrs. Billings said, sniffing. "Crippled for life, that wonderful, vital young woman."

Emma looked up at her father for an answer, but he had none to give. He hadn't quite thought of the young woman in the hospital bed as a heroine. Certainly not a role model. In fact, he wasn't aware that he had ever heard of her before Mrs. B had asked him to visit. He didn't even know her first name. All he knew was that people called her by her initials, and she apparently had quite a following, which came as a surprise to him because she seemed so alone in her hospital room, refusing visitors and keeping the truth from her own father.

"She isn't going to die, is she, Daddy?" Emma quizzed, wanting reassurance, obviously stricken with the sense of doom she heard in Mrs. Billings's voice.

But Mrs. Billings answered for him. "She might not like living anymore," she said, returning to the stove.

"Why?" Emma looked to her father, and he put his hand gently on the top of her head.

He dropped to his haunches to explain, although he was having a little trouble with it himself. "This woman, B. J. Dolliver, was very active and traveled around the world taking photographs, running after big stories to be printed in newspapers and magazines. An now, well, she won't be able to do any of those things when she has to walk with crutches, and Mrs. Billings means that, for B. J. Dolliver, not being able to do all the things she loves to do is very sad. Maybe.''

"But there's lots of things she can still do, isn't there?" Emma questioned. "She can still see and hear, can't she? And read books? And watch television and walk around with crutches? And she could swing on a swing if she wanted to, couldn't she? And go down a slide and ride on a merry-go-round? If she wanted to?"

"Yes, she could, if she wanted to. But maybe she isn't interested in those things."

"But maybe if she tried them, she might like them, and then she would be happy, wouldn't she?"

He ruffled her hair. "You're very wise, Emma, and I'm proud of you. Maybe someday you'll get to meet B. J. Dolliver and you can tell her how great it is to be alive."

It was a casual statement to appease the curiosity of a child, and he couldn't begin to think that what he said was in any way applicable to the reality of the situation. It was obvious B. J. Dolliver wasn't even thinking of dying. She was going to tangle aggressively with fate and challenge providence. She had sounded determined to battle with her own body to force it to do what the medical profession said it would never again be able to do.

Obviously, she was not making it easy for the hospital staff, including her own physician. She had locked herself into a self-imposed capsule, holding everyone else away and struggling with desperate ineffectiveness to make liars of her doctors.

He wondered what B. J. Dolliver was going to do when she discovered that the medical profession knew better than she did, and that she would never walk again without crutches, and that she damned well would never run again or wield a tennis racket or chase down a combat soldier to get his picture. He wondered how she was going to take that, accept defeat and the hopelessness of her future as she envisioned it.

Alone. Facing it alone.

As he sat down to dinner, B. J. Dolliver filled his thoughts, and he discovered with just a minimum of soul-searching that he wanted to be there when she finally fell. He wanted to be there to catch her and hold her and tell her there were still things to live for.

Chapter Two

The telephone awakened him late in the night.

Hamish answered the ring quickly, before he was entirely awake. There was a telephone next to his bed and getting late-night calls wasn't uncommon in his line of work.

"Hi, Hamish," she said, and he dropped back on his pillow and groaned. He hadn't seen B. J. Dolliver for three days.

He glanced at his clock. "It's nearly 3:00 a.m.," he said, his voice still hoarse from sleep. "Where did you get my number?" He vaguely remembered giving her his card, but he believed she'd thrown it away.

"It's in the yellow pages under righteous," she quipped.

"What's wrong, B.J.? Why are you calling me so late?"

"I'm moving out of this place," she said. According to his fuzzy calculations, he had been visiting her every few days for nearly four weeks.

"Well, that's great. They're letting you go. You must be making good progress. How's the arm?" Although she'd never appeared to accept his offer of friendship, she'd never followed through on her threat to have the hospital staff remove him.

"Arm's getting better all the time."

"Where are you going?"

"I get to pick the place." He sensed a warning in the way her voice lilted up slightly on the last word, and he tried to shake off the fog of deep sleep that clouded his thoughts.

"So, have you made a decision?" he asked, wishing he could think clearly.

"I thought maybe you'd drop by and help me with that."

"When?"

"In about an hour, preferably."

"No more games, B.J. It's nearly three in the morning. What's the problem?"

"The problem is, there is no problem!" she cried. "It's all cut-and-dried, all decided! The medical profession is turning me loose. They've given me all these wonderful places to choose from for the next phase of my life. Beautiful places. One of them even has a swimming pool."

"I don't understand," he mumbled, pinching his eyes closed, wanting to know what was causing her distress.

"You wouldn't. I don't even know why I called you. See you around, Hamish."

"Wait!" He was afraid she would hang up and he couldn't allow that. He forced his mind to work, threw the covers back and turned to sit with his legs over the side of his old four-poster bed. "Give me time to dress. It'll take me half an hour to drive—"

"No...that won't be necessary," she said, but her voice was suddenly soft and hoarse.

"What?"

"Forget I called." He thought he heard a slight warble,

but he couldn't be sure. "Go back to sleep," she said, clearing her throat. He closed his eyes again and stood on the cool hardwood floor, rotating his shoulders to stretch his muscles as he dressed. "Hamish?" she questioned when he didn't answer.

"I'll be there," he said.

"No. I didn't mean it. Really, I didn't mean it. I was just...it was stupid...I'll never forgive you if you embarrass me by coming down here in the middle of the night. Besides, they just gave me a sleeping pill, and I won't even know you're here."

"You wouldn't have called if you weren't in trouble," he replied.

"Trouble?" she chided, but he detected a lack of force in her words. "You know me better than that. Now, go back to sleep. I'm going there myself."

"No, I don't think so."

"Please," she whispered. "Please don't be so damned...serious. I swear I'll never forgive you if you come down here at this time of night. I swear it."

He was torn with indecision, and then she hung up, saying, "I'm getting very sleepy," slurring her words slightly. "Very...sleepy."

He sat on the edge of the bed, feeling the cool draft on his feet. He was now wide-awake, agitated because once again she had tied him in knots, and wondered what he should do. He knew in his heart that she had been desperate to call him. She had never called him before.

He dressed quickly and slipped out of the house into the pre-dawn night. As he drove to the hospital, he blamed her stubborn, prickly pride for how she had reached out in despair with one hand while insulting him and pushing him away with the other. Then he thought about her early life, the trauma of her mother's death, being neglected by an insensitive father. He remembered the fear he had seen in her eyes and suspected there were probably very few people she had learned to trust in her life. And yet she had become a strong, accomplished woman. He understood why she had wrapped her pride around herself like insulation from a hurtful world.

He fought a sense of foreboding while he drove to the hospital. He had a sickening feeling in his gut. She needed him. She must, he realized, to have called him like this.

He prayed for serenity and guidance while he hastened to her room. When he strode through the door, he found her sitting on the side of her bed, dangling her feet over the edge. She was beautiful, her hair tousled from sleep, the scar on her face fading to pink.

She wore one of those ugly, thin hospital gowns pulled off one shoulder, her legs bare to midthigh. Her muddy green eyes looked up at him. "You came," she whispered, and then her eyes closed, and he knew he was in trouble. He wanted to touch her. He wanted very badly to touch her. "There," she rasped, pointing to a messy array of colored pamphlets.

He reached out and picked up several, then glanced quickly through them. They were promotional brochures, glossy and brightly colored, featuring modern buildings, Victorian mansions, sterile bedrooms and lots of people in residence—people in wheelchairs, most of them with white hair, wrinkled skin and empty eyes.

He looked questioningly at her, fanning the brochures out in front of him. She nodded, her eyes filling with tears. "Nursing homes," she confirmed. "I get to choose one."

"Oh, my God," he gasped, dropping them onto the bed. He picked her up impulsively, as if she were a child, and when he felt her good arm go around his neck, he held her against him, her legs dangling free over his thighs, her face nestled in his neck. He turned in a slow circle, burying his face in her hair, and he let his heart ache while his body reveled in holding her. Absently, he pulled her gown closed over her back and held it there with his arms clasped around her. She felt frail and soft. Helpless. Warm. "Am I hurting you?" he whispered into her tangled hair. She shook her head a little wildly, and he felt wetness on his neck. "They can't send you away. You're going to get well," he whispered. "I won't let them do this to you. I won't let it happen."

Lost in comforting her and not wanting to let her go, he failed to notice how much time had passed until his arms felt the strain, and he finally returned her to the bed.

Her mouth was open slightly in obvious bewilderment, and he noticed how very kissable it looked. She had felt good pressed against him. She had felt damned good in his arms. He might have intended to give her comfort, but there was something deeper going on, and he recognized it all too well.

Quickly, he went to the closet and got her robe. He helped her get her injured arm into it. She kept her face lowered, obviously unwilling to let him see the tears she had likely fought not to shed in the first place.

"I have money," she said finally in her husky voice. "But I have nowhere to go. I can't take care of myself yet."

"Your father? Another relative? A friend?"

"No. No, I can't. Nobody would want me. I can't."

"We'll think of something, dear lady," he said, sitting alongside her on the bed. "We'll think of something."

"There's a convalescent center nearby, but it's all old people. They're all old. And I'm young, damn it. I've never needed anyone to take care of me. Never. I don't know what I'm going to do now."

"We'll find somewhere else," he reassured her.

"They've given up on me because I haven't made any progress lately. They think this is as good as I'm going to get. They're wrong. I'm going to get better. I'm going to get much, much better.''

"I believe you."

"You're the only one who does."

"Well, you called me," he sighed. "I didn't think you had kept the number."

She reached over with her left hand and used it to raise her limp right hand. There, written across her palm was his telephone number in ballpoint pen, smudged but legible, as if she had traced over it many times. "It's been there for weeks. Every day after my bath, I go over it again so it won't fade, so I'll always know where it is," she said.

Something lurched in his chest when he looked at her palm and thought of her outlining his phone number in her flesh every day and only calling him in the middle of the night when she was desperate. He raised her chin and looked into her glistening eyes. He saw that something in her had been defeated, and even though she had consistently rejected his efforts to help, he was now apparently her last resort.

He remembered the day Maralynn had died. He'd stayed with her all night long, sitting beside her bed. At the time he'd felt there was something bleak and desperate about a hospital in the middle of the night when sounds echoed only occasionally through the halls, amplified by the absence of people talking and moving about. He'd thought then that it was best to be asleep. It had seemed to him that if you didn't get to sleep before darkness descended on the hospital, you would not get to sleep at all.

He tried to imagine what B. J. Dolliver had gone through, and he decided she had agonized for a long time before she'd called him. He suspected her pride would not have let her call unless she was overwhelmed with fear.

"I can't stay here," she said.

"When did you get the pamphlets?"

"Two days ago. They expected me to make a decision by now. I think I'm supposed to be gone. I told them I could pay for the room if my insurance doesn't cover it."

"Why did you wait so long to call me?" he asked.

He watched her raise her chin in a weak reflection of defiance. "I vowed I would not call you at all."

"But what about that?" He gestured toward her limp hand with his telephone number written on her skin.

"I never intended to use it," she said after a long silence.

He sighed. "Your destructive pride driving you to the wall." He looked at her. "How do you expect me to arrange something in less than twenty-four hours?"

"You believe in miracles. I know you do. I don't know anybody else who believes in miracles," she said in a tearful, jerky voice.

Deep in thought, he stuffed his hands into his pockets and ambled to the windows. There was only one place he wanted to take her, and it was probably the last place she ought to be. He could let her sleep on the daybed in his office, and probably Mrs. Billings and the children could help. He didn't think some people in his congregation would like the idea, but then he didn't like the idea much himself. And although Mrs. Billings would be thrilled at first to have her heroine under their roof, he was sure B.J.'s rough edges would wear her welcome thin in quick order.

It was an idea bordering on insanity, he realized. She wasn't his responsibility. She was dangerous to him, in fact, a threat to the orderliness of his full, rich life. How could he even think of taking her home, now that he found himself attracted to her?

Still, there seemed nowhere else for her to go. She was terrified of a nursing home, so terrified that she had finally swallowed her pride and called him. What he feared most was her feeling defeated and helpless and taking an easy exit to avoid a fate worse than death. He remembered Mrs. B repeating Deborah's fears, although until now he had assumed they were both mistaken. He had to know.

"What if I can't find a place?" he asked.

"You said you would." For the first time, he sensed the flatness in her husky voice.

"If I can't, then what?" She hesitated. He listened closely to her voice, to each nuance and pause. His back to her, he kept his eyes shut to sharpen his perceptions of her. "Then what?" he insisted, not kindly.

"I won't go," she said, and he barely heard her.

"If I walk out this door today and say I can't help you, what will you do?" She didn't answer. "What will you do?" he demanded, letting frustration edge his words.

"I'll wave goodbye," she said, and although he recognized she was trying to be flippant, he caught another meaning in her choice of words, and he wondered exactly what his options were. Was he being manipulated? Would she put a finish to the job if he left her now? It seemed unlikely since she was so determined to get well. But what if he was wrong?

He opened his eyes to see the shadowy street below illuminated by splashes of gold from streetlights and faint reflections from the pink horizon in the east. Dawn was breaking. Trying to focus his thoughts, he rubbed his chin, then clasped his hands.

What should I do? What's my direction?

He reminded himself that he'd never been good at analyzing things, always ending up going in circles. The bald, fearsome truth was that he found it exciting—the thought of having B.J. close by in his home, under his protection, within reach of his touch. He hoped that it was his heart and mind speaking and not some other part of his anatomy.

He thought about Mrs. Billings having been a registered nurse most of her life, and he thought about the medical aids still in the house from his wife's illness—the tub rails, the upstairs hall rails and the wheelchair ramp stored in the barn that served as a garage. They were all there, the pieces that fitted as if meant to be.

When he turned to look at B.J., she was lying still. Finally asleep, he thought. He left her then and found the cafeteria open. He drank some coffee, walked around the neighboring streets, watched the sunrise and finally visited the chapel.

The halls were alive with the usual daytime sights and sounds when he returned to the vicinity of B.J.'s room. He wanted to talk to her physician, Dr. Wahler, who was not available.

The nurse he had met before was at the station, however, and as free as ever with her opinions. "She's being unreasonable," she said, shaking her head sharply. "It isn't a retirement home. It's a convalescent center. Of course there are elderly people, but not entirely, and therapy can be continued. Or private nursing can be arranged for her."

Hamish didn't like the way she frowned and pursed her lips, as if she was exasperated with her patient.

"She can probably afford it, three shifts a day, installation of aids in her condo." Her shrug was like a dismissal, and Hamish left her to call Mrs. B.

"I hope you'll bring her home," she suggested.

"There are other places for her to go. I don't know whether to recommend a convalescent center or private care," he told her.

"Neither is a good choice," Mrs. B insisted. "Both are for people who have no one."

"Well, that fits B. J. Dolliver pretty well. And it's her choice to be alone," he reminded her.

"So, who's the one person who has successfully ignored her no-visitor plea?" she challenged.

When he did not reply, she charged ahead, "Who's the one person she called when she needed help? Who's there now trying to help her?"

He inhaled deeply and closed his eyes against the obvious. It was what he wanted. And feared. B.J. in his home day and night, needing him, goading and arousing him while she healed under his family's care. B.J.—making him feel alive, so alive.

"It's your decision, Hamish, but if you're taking votes, you know which way mine goes," Mrs. B said.

"We'll see," he muttered before he broke the connection.

Back in her room, B.J. once again sat on the edge of her bed, waiting for him. He patiently explained the benefits of the options available to her, avoiding her eyes and finally rising abruptly from the chair and walking to the window, turning his back on her again so that she wouldn't see that his heart wasn't in what he was advising.

"It's your decision," he said at last.

"Go away," she rasped.

Rudeness. Now that was something he could handle. "So we're back to that, are we?" he charged, swinging around to face her.

"Just go away. Who needs you?"

He moved to her bedside and saw what a fragile mask she was presenting to him, and something melted behind his ribs and seeped, burning, into his midsection. "You do," he said finally.

"I never needed you," she whispered, but her lips quivered, almost imperceptibly.

"I think you do," he insisted, swallowing hard against the urge to gather her in his arms.

"I can't go to one of those…places. I can't. I won't."

"You can have private care in the comfort of your condo."

"Strangers, all of them, changing shifts every eight hours, talking to me as if I'm six years old. Breakfast at eight, lunch at twelve. Oops, can't fix dinner, that's for the next shift. Prodding and poking, taking my blood pressure in the middle of the night. What kind of home life would that be? They would hate me. I'm not an agreeable patient. It wouldn't work."

He stared hard at the tangle of her hair. Her face was turned away from him. "Okay," he said, more harshly than he intended. "Okay," he amended, softening, "you can come home with me."

She searched his face with despair and anxiety. She wondered if he saw what she felt, if he sensed how many sleepless nights she had tossed, dreading the dawn. Did he see that she was as near to defeat as she had ever been? Certainly she hadn't tried to hide her wariness, but then she had called him, and that was because she had grown curiously attached to him. God knew, she didn't want to trust anyone.

She watched him, the handsome, quiet strength in his face, the way he stood before her, unaware of how substantial and real he appeared, the only solid person in her life.

"Yeah, I'll go home with you," she said softly.

She stiffened when she saw a flash of regret, then thought suddenly that he was going to find a way to waltz around his decision. But the dreaded words did not come. If he thought he had made a mistake inviting her to his house, he wasn't going to retract his offer.

Her body still tingled with the heady experience of being swept up in his arms when he'd charged in like an avenging angel at four o'clock in the morning. Now, she

longed to be close to him, to feel the soothing power of
his tenderness.

"There will be conditions," he told her, his voice low,
but not soft. This was a time for firmness and resolution,
it seemed, a time for promises to be made.

"I'll do whatever you say," she conceded softly before
he realized what she had said. He would never know the
damage to her precious pride, she realized.

"You will give me your word," he said, "your solemn
and sacred word that you will be courteous and sensitive
with my children and Mrs. Billings. And that you will not
insult, or in any way offend, a single member of my congregation." She looked at him in mute misery, trying to
hang on to the self-sufficiency that had deserted her. "I
promise to take good care of you," he added, but his voice
was little more than a whisper. "I will do the best I can."

She felt the trembling in her chin before she felt the
hated tears spring into her eyes, then she dropped her head
and felt her body convulse in sobs. It was her surrender
although she wasn't sure exactly what it was she was sur-
rendering to. Tenderness? Trusting herself to the care of
another? The loss of her independence? Was she going to
find his care an alternate imprisonment, second only to
three shifts of paid professionals in her own condo?

He came to her and held her against him, stroking her
hair as she wept into his shirt, and she succumbed to his
reassurance. For the first time in her life, she felt the full
weight of her body and spirit being shared by another.

"You'll be free to come and go as you please. We'll
make sure you can continue your therapy. We'll help you
get well. It won't be the best of accommodations, but at
least you won't have to worry about steps. You can help
out around the house if you want to, whatever you can
manage from your wheelchair. And you don't have to be

nice to me. You can be as insulting and rude as you like with me.''

She pounded her good fist against his chest. "Damn you," she cried between sobs. "You're the damnedest man I ever met.''

"We won't make you go to church, either," he added as she pulled away from him and her sobs began to lessen. "And you don't have to pray if you don't want to," he said. She wanted to scoff at that. She knew he wouldn't be able to live up to that promise.

She took one last weak swing at his arm. "You are the most infuriating human being. I can't wait for the day when I can walk away from your house and tell you where to stick it.'' Her words came from habit and confusion, and a kind of familiar shame because she was being despicably weak.

He laughed and ruffled her tangled hair. "Then you've given me your word? And we're checking you out of here?''

"Yes, yes, yes," she replied with renewed hope. "We have to stop and rent a wheelchair first. The crutches are mine. And I don't have any clothes to wear. They cut me out of the ones I was wearing when I was brought in.''

"Like taking a new baby home," he teased.

She didn't like his reference, but she ignored it. She wanted to get far away from the hospital as fast as possible. "The key to my condo is in my purse. Maybe you could pick up a few things for me? It isn't far.''

"I can handle that," he said laughing. She thought she should be angry with him, but he was so damnably endearing. Most likely he would get all the wrong things, but she simply gave him the key.

Hamish Chandler had confounded, entertained, infuriated and motivated her from the moment she first opened her eyes and found him studying her face. She had fought him every minute, every inch of the way, over the past few weeks because it was her nature to fight for her independence and her achievements and any threat to them. And at the same time, she had found herself baffled that she could not imagine getting on with her life without his being a part of it.

The man was an enigma, and she wondered why she was so oddly attracted to him. Probably, she thought, because the car accident had addled her brain as well as damaged her body. And now she was going to his house because she had nowhere else to go.

She had seemed to come alive once the decision was made, although there seemed little of the feisty scrapper left in her, Hamish thought, as he drove to her condo.

His call to Mrs. B had been happily received. Things at home were even now being prepared for their new houseguest. He wondered if it was possible to prepare his family for B. J. Dolliver's interesting personality and how long she would be able to abide by the conditions he had set down.

When he arrived at his destination, he let himself into B.J.'s condo and was fascinated by what he found. Photographs had been enlarged and framed in shiny chrome to decorate her walls. Awards were propped haphazardly on her dresser; clippings were in messy piles in the dining room and in her bedroom. He looked through some of them, then placed them carefully in a suitcase. Maybe it would give B.J. something to do, sorting them, reminding herself how good she was and what she would one day go back to.

The condo was an expensive place, and her furniture was exotic and eclectic, obviously collected from around the world. He took two large framed photos off the bedroom wall, wrapped them in a coverlet from her bed and carried them to his car trunk. He would hang them in his house so that she would feel more at home.

In the bedroom, he went through her dresser drawers and closet, trying to remember the kinds of things a woman needed and liked. He eventually filled two suitcases and then a grocery bag with shoes.

It dawned on him as he was packing that she was not going to be impressed with his house, not when she was accustomed to the luxury she had surrounded herself with. Maybe her long stay in the hospital would have dulled her expensive tastes, he thought. All her possessions looked costly, fashionable contemporary pieces mixed with beautiful antiques and exotic-looking imports. And there was the hot tub in the screened deck off her bedroom.

No, she wasn't going to be very happy with his home.

On the way back, he stopped to pick up the electrically powered wheelchair that had been reserved for her by Dr. Wahler. When he finally got to the hospital, he carried in the overnight bag so B.J. could get dressed. He didn't expect her to remove each item while he stood there, but that was exactly what she did, flinging bra, panties, blouse, skirt, comb and brush, sandals, deodorant and makeup down on the bed. "Well, I see you were in the right place at least," she said wryly. "But I don't usually wear lacy underwear when there isn't anyone to impress."

"I thought Mrs. Billings might have to help you undress," he retorted. He didn't want to hear that she had lacy underwear to impress a man. He didn't want to think of her with another man. He tried to concentrate on how welcome it was to hear her displaying a little of her old abrasive spirit.

"By the way," he added, "I had intended for you to sleep on the daybed in my office, but that simply won't work. You'll take over my bedroom, and I'll stay in the office. I hope you won't mind."

"But it's your bedroom. Why should *I* mind?"

"My bedroom is upstairs."

"But I can't...how will I—"

"I'll have to carry you up and down," he said, and then he looked away as curious sensations gripped him. He didn't want to feel the heat that was coursing through him. He didn't want to acknowledge how pleasant it had been to hold her against him and that what he was feeling for her was more than compassion.

Chapter Three

When B.J. saw his car, she knew there was going to be a lot of adjusting on her part. It reminded her of an old weathered hull, clean, big as sin, dull tan marred by rust corrosion along the bottom of the doors and fenders. Inside, it was spotless and worn, and when she looked around, thinking she deserved a medal for holding her tongue, he grinned at her and said, "It came with the rectory. You'll like it. Smooth ride. Like sitting on a cloud."

It was a smooth ride, and she could barely hear the engine running once he managed to get it started.

She hadn't thought to ask where Kolstad was, hadn't really cared. It was simply the place where Hamish lived and worked. In truth, he didn't seem like a pastor at all. Not that she had had much contact with clergy in her years of living with a father who worshiped athletic prowess above all, and thought spirituality referred to poltergeists.

Hamish was a gorgeous man to look at, and she would never in all her life forget the magnificent charge she'd felt when he held her in his arms. Of course, she couldn't tell him how his gentle ways affected her, because they touched something so deep in her she ached with it. No man in her life had ever made her feel so threatened, or so feminine. She had missed him between visits, and hated admitting that she did. Life in the hospital had taken on a chill when he wasn't around. She'd felt adrift, missing his laughter and his confidence and the infuriating way he had of fielding her insults as if she were an amusing child punching at shadows.

Kolstad was only a half hour from downtown and the hospital, a straight shot down a country highway from the freeway. First she saw the cornfields, then the suburban housing developments and finally the small old town blooming within the ever-growing suburbia. On the east edge of the town, they pulled into the driveway of an old, squat, prairie-style farmhouse surrounded by a chain-link fence, precisely cut lawn and acres of hay field all around it.

Behind the house were two sheds, one large and apparently also serving as a garage, and the other smaller, converted into a children's playhouse of some sort. Two little girls ran to meet Hamish, stopping only to struggle with the latch on the chain-link gate and then flying into him as he came around the back of the car.

He hunkered down to hug them both, then stood with one in each arm. He nodded toward her, and something caught in her chest at how tenderly he held his children and how much they adored him.

When he set them down, he pulled open the passenger door. "You'll have to tell them your name," he said. "I never did ask."

She frowned at the lie, then looked at them. "B.J.," she said.

"No, your real name," he insisted with his beguiling soft laughter.

"It's just B.J.," she repeated.

"Belinda Jean? Begonia Jasmine? C'mon, let's have it."

"Brenda Jane," she said reluctantly. "I hate it."

"Brenda Jane is a beautiful name," he countered. He spread a hand on the top of each little girl's head, the taller one with the dark curly hair and the smaller one with the straight blond strands. "This is Emma, and this is Annie. Say hello to Brenda, girls."

Emma moved forward, her eyes wide with innocent curiosity. "Hi," she said. "My daddy said you have crutches."

Annie hung back, fingers in her mouth, peeking around her father's khaki trousers. He just stood there like a proud dad and grinned. It was plain to see which of the girls had his personality.

"Stand back," Hamish said, pulling Emma away from her. "Brenda has to get out and stand up on her own. It's very hard for her. Remember I told you she was hurt in a car accident?"

The girls stepped back in solemn obedience and clutched at his trousers, Emma at a pocket, Annie on a seam. B.J. didn't particularly like having an audience to watch her awkward efforts, but nobody laughed. When she was perched on the edge of the seat with both feet on the ground, Emma stepped forward with her hand extended. "Can I help?"

B.J. looked at the innocent eagerness in the chocolate brown eyes, and smiled. "Sure." She took the little girl's hand. "Pull," she said. Emma pulled and B.J. pushed until she was standing.

"Okay," Hamish said, then lifted her and cradled her in his arms. "I'll take you to see Mrs. Billings."

The girls ran ahead, hopping and skipping and turning in circles. They opened the gate and then the back door.

Hamish finally set her down on a wood chair at a wood table covered with oil cloth in an old-fashioned run-down kitchen. She hadn't seen anything like it since she was a child visiting an ancient relative who still lived "in the country." The only modern convenience she saw was a toaster.

Mrs. Billings was in her fifties now. Her hair was graying, and she wore polyester pants and a paisley overblouse that failed to hide her barrel waist. She smiled and jiggled as she spread her arms wide and gave B.J. a long, gentle hug. "Lemonade?" she offered. "Coffee?"

Not much had changed, B.J. thought. Here again was Deborah's beloved aunt with her round, beaming face and warm, laughing eyes she remembered so well.

"We're gonna get kittens," Emma said. "Rainbow has 'em in her tummy."

B.J. smiled at Emma. "Are you going to have lemonade?"

"I don't like lemonade. It's too sour. Do you like kittens?"

"I don't know. I never had one."

The child's brown eyes widened to saucers and her mouth dropped open. "You never had a kitten!" Her response connoted a ghastly deprivation—worse, it seemed, than her accident.

"What's so bad about that?" B.J. challenged. "I never missed having one."

But Emma's astonishment knew no bounds. "Didn't you ever hold one?"

"No, I don't think so. Kittens weren't my thing. Never cared for the little buggers," she said.

"Never cared for a *kitten!*" Emma made a face to share her horror with Annie, whose blue eyes reflected concern as she, too, shook her head slowly. They were clearly in deep sympathy with her problem.

As B.J. rolled her eyes, she caught Mrs. Billings's chuckle and felt for a moment as if she had been dropped into another world. Little girls liked juvenile hard rock and dressing Barbie dolls. Kittens were surely passé. Why weren't they experimenting with makeup or watching television or stealing coins off the dresser like normal kids did? B.J. wondered. "I'll have lemonade," she said to Mrs. Billings.

"It's really sour," Emma warned, scrunching up her face.

"So am I. We'll get along fine," she said, watching Hamish come through the door with her suitcases.

"These are Brenda's things," he announced.

"Damn it, I'm B.J."

"Don't swear in front of the children," he said softly, leaning toward her.

"Sorry. I'm not Brenda. I've never been Brenda. It's the name of some soap opera person my mother liked before I was born," she muttered.

"It's a nice name, very feminine. Like you. Sometimes," he said, and then added, "Brenda Jane."

She rolled her eyes. "Dear Lord, help me," she sighed without reverence, then she heard his soft laugh.

"Catching on already?" he quipped.

Annie crawled up on a chair, folded her arms on the edge of the table, rested her chin in the middle of them and silently stared at her. Emma flitted around the room chattering about first grade, which she had just started, about riding the school bus like the big kids, about playing Chinese checkers and hating pineapple because it stung her mouth. She showed B.J. her loose tooth and said she didn't have to change clothes after school today because B.J. was coming to stay and so it was okay to leave her good clothes on.

"My daddy's going to sleep in his office," she announced, skipping on one foot, holding the toes of the other one behind her.

"Is that all you do is talk?" B.J. asked. "You never stop talking."

"Pretty much. Mrs. Billings calls me a chatterbox. Daddy said once I said my first word I never shut up." Her high-pitched laughter sailed around the room. "That's silly, 'cause I don't talk when I sleep, or in church. Or when I'm supposed to be quiet in school."

"Why do you talk so much?" B.J. asked, mesmerized by this miniature version of the reverend, with all his joy and open laughter bubbling out of her like soapsuds.

"There's lots to say," she said, hopping in a circle. "I bet you can't do this."

"I could a few weeks ago. Someday I'll be able to do it again."

Hamish was on another trip from the car, and now her suitcases and whatever else he had brought from her condo were upstairs in his bedroom, which was to be her bedroom now. He had done a surprisingly thorough job of packing the overnight bag he'd brought to the hospital, and it had fascinated her that he knew a woman's personal needs so well. She watched him move smoothly around the house, admiring his broad shoulders and the grace of his strides. She imagined he must have had more than his share of women before he was married. She wondered if there was someone now.

Unwilling to pursue that train of thought, she smiled at Annie, a forced smile, but the little girl did not respond. Blue eyes followed her every movement as if she were being visually traced. She tried winking, but Annie wasn't buying it. B.J. made a face, but except for a slight narrowing of Annie's eyes for a moment, it cut no ice with the little girl.

"She seems like a happy kid," B.J. said, switching her

attention to Emma, who was now trying to balance on a thin line, which snaked through the worn vinyl pattern on the floor.

"Oh my, yes," Mrs. Billings answered. "This is a happy family in spite of their loss." The older woman smiled at Emma, then reached over quickly and tickled Annie, who giggled and squirmed and then returned to her watchdog posture.

B.J. couldn't remember ever feeling carefree and safe, not like the skinny little girl with the frizzy brown hair. She couldn't remember it ever being all right just to be a girl, to be feminine, to like pretty colors, to wear a frilly pink dress like Annie did. She couldn't remember when she wasn't competing for her father's attention, competing with other athletes, competing with his business, proving she was as good as all those guys he admired so much, proving she could be a part of his business because she was smart and interested and a good athlete herself.

Looking back as far as she could, she didn't think she had ever been glad enough to see her father to jump on him. And anyway, he would have flung her aside for a fool, making an uncontrolled lunge like that. She wondered if he had ever carried her in his arms or spread his fingers over the top of her head like a loving anointment. She couldn't even recall if he had ever spoken to her in other than his gruff wrestler's growl. Greeting his friends had been a test to see who staggered the least from a knuckle punch to the shoulder.

It was easier, of course, when she'd been a teenager because the guys liked her looks, and she put her heart and soul into gymnastics and tennis so that her father could show her off to his friends. That was when the boy thing started. "Yeah, steal a kiss from my girl and she'll cuff you to Timbuktu," he had said to her date one night.

He had laughed and bragged to his friends when the

boys called her in droves, and although in eleventh grade she'd had a wild crush on Leonard Holmes, she flirted with all the athletes to avoid an intimacy with him that scared her to her core. When Patrick Dolliver bragged about his "little heartbreaker" and his "helluva athlete for a woman," she knew she had found the secret to competing successfully for his attention.

Now she was twenty-seven years old and had never had a serious relationship with a man. Though she'd casually dated many men, she'd never let anyone get too close, no matter how empty she felt when her women friends went off with their one important man, who held them close and smiled into their eyes in front of everyone.

"I've so been looking forward to seeing you again," Mrs. Billings said suddenly, as if she had been holding back her enthusiasm for the past half hour. The gush of attention startled B.J. "Deb talks about you all the time," Mrs. B said. "We've been following your career, you know. I think you're the bravest woman I've ever known. I so wish Deborah could be more like you."

B.J. was dumbfounded. "Oh? Well, thank you, Mrs. B. I've always admired Deb for how, well, how normal she is!"

B.J. didn't expect Deb's aunt to understand and merely smiled when Mrs. B gave her a quizzical look.

"Your photography is outstanding," Mrs. B said then. "I'm so glad you brought some with you. Pastor is hanging them now in your bedroom."

"What? I don't understand."

"The framed photos he hauled in a few minutes ago. I recognized one of them as yours."

"Where is he?" B.J. asked. "I want to talk to him." She hadn't noticed what he was hauling in. She had only been aware that he had been traipsing through the kitchen, carting her belongings—*his* choice of her belongings.

Mrs. Billings rose from her chair and ambled away. "Pastor, B.J. wants to talk to you," she called. "I don't know what it's about. The pictures, I think."

Hamish was towering over B.J. a few minutes later. "What have you done?" she demanded, ignoring his grin.

He simply scooped her up and headed into the next room. It was a formal dining room with a leaded window looking out to an enclosed front porch. An antique dining-room set graced the middle of the room. He carried her to the right, through an archway of varnished wood flanked by built-in, glass-doored cabinets. Opposite was a staircase hugging the wall, its varnished wood gleaming.

He ascended three steps to the landing, then turned and carried her up the rest of the flight. She wanted to glare at him, but found it too interesting being so close, smelling his aftershave and feeling his hard, broad chest against her body. He carried her as though she were a baby—carefully and with little effort.

At the top of the stairs, he turned left into a bedroom with an antique double bed, its posts reaching nearly to the ceiling. He set her on the edge of the bed facing away from the double windows, then stepped back toward the wall where two of her framed photographs hung side by side.

"What have you done?" she demanded again.

"I thought they would make you feel more at home," he said. "I figured if you didn't like them, you wouldn't have had them on your wall."

She felt exposed, as if he had stepped through the fragile door to her private space, reminding her of what she had been before the accident. "I liked them where they were—" She stopped herself before the insult rushing to her lips could erupt.

How ironic, she thought fleetingly, that being here with

this man in this oh-so-very-comfortable and very old house should trigger such vulnerability in her.

Hamish's arms dropped to his sides, and his smile vanished, replaced by an expression so stricken, she was immediately contrite.

"I'm sorry, Brenda," he said softly, reaching for the photograph closest to him. "I didn't mean to offend you, or upset you." He took it down gently and propped it against the wall, then reached for the next one. "I thought you might feel more comfortable with something of your own to look at when you woke up in the morning." He carefully took the other picture down, then reached for the folded coverlet she recognized as the one from her bed at home. He laid it beside her.

"No. Stop," she cried, unnerved by the strangeness of all that was happening to her, appalled that she had felt so threatened by what had in reality been his thoughtfulness.

"I'll take them back to your condo tomorrow," he said. "It was presumptuous of me. I should have asked first."

She let herself fall back on the soft bed and covered her eyes with her left hand. She felt the coverlet under her head and reached up to gather it in her hand, pulling it over her, hugging it against her face. "No," she told him. "Leave them. You're right. It will be nice to have my things here." She was shaken, though, and her voice came out huskier than usual, tempered by her roiling emotions, none of which made sense, even to her.

Then he was hovering over her, his hands on either side of her head. "It's all right. I'll take them back. I don't mind. I'm just sorry I made a bad choice." His gaze wandered around her hairline and down to her mouth. "I want you to be comfortable here, Brenda Jane. I know it isn't what you're used to. There's nothing new or fine or expensive here, and it's pretty dark in here most of the time. I was afraid you would find it dreary and I couldn't think of any other way to brighten it for you." He focused his blue gaze on her eyes again. "I want to take good care of you while you're here," he said softly, smiling with a warmth she knew she didn't deserve.

He was reaching around her defenses and touching something deep inside that ached with a strange yearning. She felt tears gathering behind her eyes and she cursed him and herself as she hugged the soft coverlet to her cheek. "I'm the one who should apologize," she whispered. "It was a really nice thing to do. It just surprised me, that's all, and when I'm surprised I sometimes attack without thinking. Please put them back up."

He looked at her skeptically, as if he thought she was patronizing him.

"Please," she said, "I want them where I can see them. And I'm sorry for—your house is nice, Hamish. It's comfortable. And it's clean. My place is never this clean."

He leaned toward her and slowly smiled, studying her face, sending a wild shot of pleasure through her. "Okay," he said, "I'll put them back up."

A little while later, Mrs. B was helping her into a nightgown for a nap before dinner. B.J. watched the woman as she took her clothes from the suitcases and put them in the chest of drawers and the closet.

"Pastor says you're determined to prove your doctor wrong," Mrs. B said as she hung up a blouse. "I sincerely hope you succeed. When I think of your life—jet-setting about and all those handsome lovers…"

"It wasn't the way it looked, Mrs. B," she said quickly, breaking her own rule. "They weren't lovers." When Mrs. B froze and stared at her, she continued, "I know what people think, but they're wrong. I was never intimate with any of them. I know how men are. They can't be trusted.

And earning their love is just too damn hard. I can get along very nicely all by myself.''

She didn't know whether to laugh or cry when Mrs. B patted her hand and shook her head. She saw understanding and sadness, respect and regret. She didn't really understand why she couldn't allow herself to get involved in an intimate relationship.

When Mrs. B left, B.J. realized she felt good about confiding in Deb's aunt, then she lay back comfortably in the high, firm, four-poster bed and looked at the familiar framed prints of her photographic work. How had Hamish known it would bring her a curious comfort to see them here?

Hamish. She still couldn't believe he was a pastor. The first thing she had noticed about him was that he didn't just sit back and stare at her with distaste or wonder what to do with his hands. He had a quiet self-confidence and a kind of serenity that was unnerving, and he had a body that would melt the resolve of an ice queen. That was what made her most suspicious, that broad chest and flat stomach, and the huge, warm hands that had repeatedly sustained her.

No minister she ever heard of had a name like Hamish Chandler. Of course, no minister she could have imagined would have copper brown hair that hung sexily over his forehead and begged a woman's touch, or blue eyes that sparkled with humor and undisguised joy. He was too handsome by far to be a clergyman, and he had kept his word and hadn't made any kind of show about praying over her.

In the nearly four weeks she had known him, she hadn't seen him clasp his hands together even once, or murmur platitudes, or give a lecture on piety. She had waited for just that behavior. But it hadn't come.

He'd seen her cry. No one had seen her cry since she

was seven and her father walked away, accusing her of blubbering when someone had hurt her feelings. She had learned early that if she wanted her father's love, she had to be *his* kind of person—strong, hard and self-sufficient. It wasn't that she hadn't wept her heart out a time or two; she had simply never allowed anyone to witness it.

Hamish Chandler had seen the wounds on her face, the ones the hospital staff at first hadn't allowed her to see. She felt them now and knew she was marred and ugly. She recalled the faces that had looked at her once she'd become aware she was in a hospital and unable to move except for her left arm. She thought about how Cecil and Ron, friends and fellow reporters from the newspaper, had avoided looking at her when they stood at the foot of her bed very early in her recuperation and wished her a speedy recovery. Hah! Did they think she was blind and stupid and missed their shocked expressions when they saw her swollen face? She'd insisted on no visitors after that.

Her looks had been important, although none of the macho athletic men in her life had meant any more than a means to impress and hold the attention of her only parent. She had been too strong and too smart to let any of them get too close to her. And none had gotten away with pushing her beyond the limits she'd set for herself. Wouldn't they all have been staggered to discover B. J. Dolliver was still a virgin? Who would believe it?

Except the man she married. *If* she ever married...

She had learned her lesson well—how to get along in an uncaring world. Her father had been an excellent teacher and role model, having made millions touting his athletic equipment stores and keeping his heart in ice. That was the valuable lesson he had taught her: never give your heart away.

And now she lay in the bed of the one man in her whole life who threatened to break that lesson.

* * *

Hamish was disappointed that B.J. wanted to eat in her room instead of joining the family for dinner. He was tempted to carry her downstairs anyway, but it was her first night in a new environment, and he let Mrs. B take her a tray. They still had the sturdy bed tray Maralynn had used during her illness.

He also made a mental note to bring out the wheelchair ramp for the back steps. It had been stored in the old barn for two years.

After the children were in bed, he tapped lightly on B.J.'s door. When she welcomed him inside, he sat in the chair to talk to her, thinking of all the times he had sat at her bedside in the hospital. Now she was sleeping in his bed, in his room, where until today he had slept nearly every night for as long as he'd been pastor of Kolstad Church.

"I came to discuss your schedule," he said.

"The medi-van will pick me up for my therapy at one-thirty, then bring me back at four."

"Hmm, I usually leave the house around eight in the morning," he told her, "but I'll come back around ten to carry you downstairs. Brenda, if you're up for it, I hope you'll plan to join us at the table for dinner after this."

But she didn't.

The next night, he went up to retrieve her tray, prepared to confront her, but he found her in a deep sleep, looking lovely and deceptively angelic, half-sitting against several pillows, the low bedside lamp backlighting the soft waves of her hair.

She had barely touched her food. Her napkin lay crumpled in her hand.

He gently pulled her forward, removed the extra pillows and then laid her down. After pulling the blanket to her shoulders, he held her left hand while he watched her slow, even breathing. He studied the delicate line of her jaw and the jagged little scar healing on her cheek, the slim, graceful column of her neck.

He brought her hand toward his face, and her small fingers curled reflexively around his thumb. Her nails were unadorned and short, but the tips were no longer rough and broken. He fought a startling sensual urge to pull her hands against his chest. It was a frightening sensation, and he tucked the small hand back under the blanket and wandered to the windows on the other side of the bed. He looked out at the driveway and the hay field next door. He hadn't felt desire for a woman for a long time.

The last time he had made love had been in this very bed. With Maralynn, before her illness precluded it. None of what had happened made sense to him, but life had often been like that in recent years.

There had been disappointment and anguish, but nothing like the violent nature of his youth. When he was troubled, he concentrated on how grateful he was for his children, his congregation and the daily adventures of his job. His own home was a happy one, and he thanked God for that every day. His precious children were healthy, their lives full of love and activity. He had a job he valued and a housekeeper who was like a caring aunt to all three of them.

There was little room in his life for this angry woman who fought against forces she couldn't hope to conquer, he told himself. And still, since the day he met her, she had consumed his thoughts.

He didn't know why she was so important to him. Maybe someday he would discover the reason. Then again, maybe she would soon be gone like a fleeting dream, and he would never know.

Before leaving her, he leaned over and kissed her forehead, acknowledging that he felt a protective surge of affection when he did so. Tomorrow, he decided, he would carry her downstairs for dinner.

Entering her room the next evening, he found B.J. with her head lolling to the side. She blinked her eyes with effort. "I'm just too tired," she murmured.

"Let me feed you, then," he said softly, brushing a fallen wave of hair off her forehead. "You need to eat." He had Mrs. B put together a tray and returned to the room where she lay exhausted, propped against the pillows. "It will be all right," he assured her. "Just open your mouth. I'll help you."

A short while later, she had eaten nearly everything he'd brought her. "No more," she whispered, and he watched as her head slowly slid to the side. As he had done the night before, he removed the tray, gently pulled the extra pillows away, tucked the covers around her shoulders and kissed her forehead before leaving.

By Sunday, Hamish realized they had established a ritual that needed to be broken. When he entered Brenda's bedroom he found her awake and alert. He set the tray in front of her.

"Closer," she said. "Set it closer. I can eat by myself today." She laid the napkin across her chest and started to eat, grinning as if she had just defeated him in a contest.

"Congratulations," he said, sitting in his usual place.

"I'm not so tired tonight since I didn't have to go for therapy," she said. "Besides, I don't know if I like your hanging around, feeding me and watching me fall asleep. What do you do anyway?" she challenged, picking up her spoon for another mouthful.

"Remove the extra pillows, pull up your blanket...and kiss you," he said.

She coughed. "You what?"

"Remove—"

"No, the last thing."

"Kiss you."

"I thought that's what you said." Her voice sounded strangled.

"On the forehead," he said, grinning.

"Oh." He watched the play of emotions on her face. "I don't usually like when people touch me," she said after a moment.

She returned her attention to the plate, where she was trying to cut into a piece of meat, but it was moving around under her fork, eluding her efforts. Hamish reached over, placed his fingers gently over hers and guided her until she cut the meat into two pieces. She frowned at him.

"Why don't you like when people touch you?" he asked. He didn't tell her he already knew about her notoriety as a heartbreaker. He didn't remind her that she had not objected when he held her in his arms the day he picked her up from the hospital. "That will never get you a husband," he said with a gentle smile.

"Not a problem," she returned quickly. "I'm not marriage material, you know."

When B.J. sat at the dinner table for the first time on Tuesday night and Hamish announced that she had to accompany the family to Meeting Night at the church on Wednesday, she snapped, "I don't want any part of your piety. Leave me here."

"I don't mean to impose our religion on you, Brenda," he explained with maddening patience. "I just don't want to leave you alone in the house. If I can't find someone to stay with you, I won't leave you here alone."

"I don't need a sitter."

"Yes, you do. What if a fire started? What if you fell or needed something?" His logic was unassailable, which infuriated her. "You simply can't be left here alone yet," he said.

"If you expect me to sit for two hours and pray…" B.J. never finished her sentence, for she happened to look into the frightened faces of the two little girls across the table. Hamish followed her gaze, then set his fork down. He reached for Emma and grasped her shoulder.

"She doesn't mean it," he said softly. "Annie? Emma? Brenda is just a little upset, but she isn't angry at us. And she would never do anything to harm us." He pushed his chair back and went to Annie, who was sitting on a big dictionary. He leaned close, put his hand on the top of her head and murmured against her cheek, "It's okay, punkin. She didn't mean to scare you."

"She's mean." The little warble struck B.J. like a carving knife in her chest. They were the first words she had heard spoken by the beautiful blond child, words flung at her in a trembling falsetto.

"She isn't mean," Hamish said. "She just sounds like it. But she isn't really mean, I promise you. She's just—" he looked up at B.J. for an instant "—rude."

"I don't like when you're rude," Emma wailed, her big brown eyes never leaving B.J. as they filled with tears.

B.J. was frozen to the chair, unable to speak or comprehend what she had done that so frightened the children. She hadn't thrown anything. She hadn't screamed or shouted. "What did I do?" she gasped finally.

"They aren't used to harsh words in our home," Hamish said, returning to his seat. "They aren't used to seeing their father attacked." Half amused, half angry, he raised an eyebrow pointedly at her, then he picked up his fork. "Eat, girls. I'll read you a story after dinner."

When dinner had ended and the girls had gone to the living room, B.J. turned to Hamish. "Wednesday is tomorrow. That only gives you twenty-four hours to find someone to stay with me," she said. "You could have given me more notice."

"I'll do my best to find someone," he replied. She waited for him to give her a well-deserved dressing-down for upsetting his daughters, but he didn't.

"I'm sorry I frightened Emma and Annie," she said, lowering her eyes. "I never realized...I won't...it won't—"

"Happen again?" he finished. She looked up. The sparkle in his eyes was not condemning. "They'll let you know if it does," he said. "But I'm afraid you aren't going to win over my younger one, no matter how good you are," he said, shaking his head. "Annie is very shy even under the best of circumstances."

Things hadn't started out very well, B.J. thought, hoping she would be capable of keeping her promise. They had to know by now that she was not only unfamiliar with the company of children, but she was unaccustomed to living in a family environment.

However, she had survived worse. She had learned harder lessons. She was capable of dealing with this new challenge, at least until she was well enough to leave.

The fear she had triggered in the little girl's eyes haunted her, though, because she remembered how much it hurt to be frightened by an adult you were supposed to be able to trust.

Chapter Four

Upon arriving home Wednesday afternoon, Hamish announced that he had been unable to find someone to "sit" with Brenda during Meeting Night.

The children were present, and B.J. had learned from the previous night's experience to tone down her reactions to Hamish's unpredictable expectations. "Did you try to find someone?" she asked in a low, hard, accusing voice.

He stepped back from her in mock shock. "Why, Brenda, do you think I *want* you there making a spectacle of yourself?"

Fighting to keep her mouth from twitching into a grin, she continued with her accusatory attack instead. "I can't believe you actually take little children to some boring two-hour prayer meeting," she said.

"It isn't just a prayer meeting," he said.

Hamish won, of course, and as six-thirty approached, he carried her out to her wheelchair, then walked at her side as she manipulated the left-hand controls to propel herself down the driveway. It looked to her as if he was getting her out of the house early so that Mrs. B could bring the children along later. Was she such an ogre?

He led her across the two lanes of asphalt country highway and down another gravel road bordered by trees. Within a few hundred feet, the trees cleared and an imposing brick hexagonal building with skylights and large stained-glass windows emerged like a misplaced acropolis.

It was a large contemporary edifice, not a small country church, and although it nestled compatibly with the trees and grassy knoll upon which it sat, B.J. thought it represented urban affluence rather than country religion. Hamish walked beside her in silence, heading for the sidewalk that divided into a stairway on the right, while a continuous concrete ribbon ascended the hill on the left.

As they passed through the main doors of the church, the sun in the western sky caught the colors in the stained glass high above and cast their reflection upon the altar on the far wall of the nave.

"It's beautiful," she said. "It's absolutely beautiful."

She saw that he was pleased. "It is, isn't it?" He held the door for her, then followed her into the narthex. "You don't have to participate if you don't want to," he said. "We're going to have a short service first. The choir's going to practice up there." He nodded at the balcony they were passing under at the back of the church. "The children will—hello, Tammy."

The young woman seemed to have appeared by magic until B.J. realized she simply fitted into the place, like one of the pleasing but plain blocks in the wall. She was pretty, like a desert beauty, tan pink and unadorned, her dark blond hair in a proper French braid, her slipover tan shirt filled out with her pregnancy.

"This is Tammy Bantz, wife of Assistant Pastor Medford Bantz. Tammy, this is Brenda Jane Dolliver," Hamish said.

"I've been wanting to welcome you, Brenda." Tammy spoke softly and smiled warmly. So very perfect for the part of a minister's wife, B.J. thought, a quiet, gentle, unassuming helpmate. So very unlike *her*.

"I have to leave you now and prepare," Hamish said.

It was on the tip of her tongue to chide him about being improperly dressed for conducting a service. Instead, she quirked a brow and eyed his wrinkled khaki shorts, dirty running shoes and faded T-shirt. He got the message, patted her shoulder and let his soft laughter rumble over her before he turned away and headed down the side aisle.

An elderly woman was waiting for him. B.J. could hear the merging and fading of their voices as they disappeared through a doorway. She could feel his power here. There was something peaceful and fascinating about his church.

"Pastor said you would be here." Tammy's soft, sweet voice interrupted her thoughts. It sounded almost like a child's voice, B.J. thought. "Would you like me to show you around?"

Not necessarily, she wanted to say, but she had promised Hamish to behave. "That's very thoughtful of you," she said instead.

"After the service," Tammy began, gesturing gracefully toward the altar, "the children will be doing different things around the building and outdoors, depending upon their ages." She swept her arm toward the hallways leading away from the narthex. "Some of the women will be working on quilts. They're to be auctioned off for the Christmas Food Shelf."

"Christmas? It's not even October."

Tammy's face lit up. "Oh, but Christmas is the most lovely time of year around here! We're already planning things." She led the way down the hall. "Some people will be doing crafts. And most of the rooms will have some activity. Lots of people are working on gifts and decorations for Christmas.''

"Some prayer meeting," B.J. muttered.

"I beg your pardon." Tammy seemed startled.

"Sorry, nothing. What goes on outside?"

"Softball. Sometimes volleyball. It's fun to watch, especially if Pastor plays," Tammy said. "Of course, it's sometimes kind of cold outside, but we're having a nice fall this year. This might be one of our last softball games, even though we have lights."

When Mrs. Billings finally arrived with the children, she suggested that B.J. wheel her chair up the side to the front to give her a clear view of the proceedings. Tammy accompanied them.

Mrs. Billings sat in the pew beside her, with the girls on Mrs. B's other side. The church filled up fast amid the murmurs of people in conversation and the sound of feet sliding along the carpeting. At seven o'clock, B.J. looked back to see that the church was about two-thirds full. She estimated that there were about two hundred men, women and children.

As the organ music began, she looked up at the oak-carved altar and the big man who appeared there in a navy blue and white vestment, his hands clasped over his flat midsection. He really did look like a genuine pastor. The sight of the stiff white collar caused a stitch in her chest.

"Good evening, friends and neighbors," Hamish said, his lovely deep baritone voice carrying over their heads. "Please join me in prayer." With the organ playing softly in the background, he raised his head, spread his palms in a gesture of invitation and began the prayer service.

She was mesmerized as he spoke, asking blessings for this and that, giving thanks, affirming that how each person conducted his or her life on an hour-to-hour basis was more important than merely going through rituals because they seemed to be required. He introduced a little boy who read something that sounded quite biblical.

After making some announcements, he gestured toward B.J. and said, "And I ask you to pray for the speedy recovery of a guest in our congregation. A young woman whom many of you may recognize has come among us to regain her health. Her name is Brenda Jane Dolliver, and she believes in miracles."

In front of hundreds of people he had done it again. He'd reached inside her and touched her, and this time he had pulled her into his life with a grasp so stout she was speechless with terror. With his irresistible power and words that created a kind of magic around her, he was drawing her inexorably into the fabric of his world.

But it was an alien world. Alien and unknown, like a mysterious and vast space, offering the kind of tenderness and care that would sap her strength and make her soft, so that when the time came for her to stand alone, she would find herself dangerously weakened instead.

Chaos erupted when the service was over. People left in every direction, singers asking for songbooks, athletes looking for baseballs, a young woman wanting a key for the craft room, an old man complaining about the coffee, children calling to friends, one frazzled woman looking for a lost child.

The scene reminded her of a playground as people gradually organized themselves, things were found, shoes were tied, hands were held. Several people came up to her, clasped her left hand and said they would pray for her full recovery. They welcomed her to the area, but cooled when she said she was staying at the pastor's house.

Tammy leaned down and whispered in her ear, "Pastor is widowed and very handsome, and some people think it's, um, well, suggestive that a young single woman would be sleeping in his house.''

"That's insane!'' B.J. erupted. "Hamish would never... How could anyone even think...? And Mrs. Billings and his daughters are there! What kind of people—''

She was interrupted by Tammy's light touch on her arm. "Don't be upset,'' she pleaded gently. "I probably shouldn't have said anything. Of course it's ridiculous. But, well, it's just appearances that count with some people.''

Mrs. Billings disappeared with the two girls, and B.J. declined Tammy's invitation to join the quilters or to check out the crafters. Instead, she had Tammy point her in the direction of the ball field.

It was a respectable ball field with a sturdy new backstop and two sets of bleachers. As she rode her chair across the grass, she saw that the group of mostly men, a few young women and a few teenage boys were already selecting their teams. When all of them had lined up on one side or another, someone shouted, "Hey, Pastor, you gonna play?''

"Do you need me?'' he called back, exiting the church at an easy jog, clad once more in shorts.

"Yeah, Velma needs a good hitter!''

He waved to B.J. as he jogged to the team at bat. "Need a pitcher, too?'' she heard him ask Velma, the team's captain.

B.J. wheeled to the bleachers, which were nearly full, and watched wistfully. In ordinary times, she'd have been in the thick of it, not sitting like a helpless fool on the sidelines. She itched to play, to wear a mitt and feel the force of the ball as it slammed into her glove. She longed to swing at the ball and feel the smack when it sailed over second base. She wanted to feel the sand under her shoes and the excitement of making a base without getting tagged. Instead, she watched. Helpless.

When Hamish came up to bat, everyone cheered, and he hit a home run on the first pitch, trotting easily around the bases until he touched third and broke into a steady hard run to get home before the ball did. He was damned good, and her heart was beating wildly from the time he stepped to the plate to the time he completed the run. She slapped her left hand over and over again on the arm of her chair and caught herself screaming for him to get the lead out.

He also pitched the first two innings, throwing and catching as if he had been doing it all his life. B.J. realized that he was far and away beyond any other player on the field. He demonstrated a powerful fluidity in his movements, like a talented and well-trained athlete. An understated athlete.

In the top of the fourth inning, he was leading off second base, flirting with the pitcher, when Annie came running from the church. The little girl tumbled on her stomach, started to get up, then buried her face in her hands and sobbed into the grass.

Hamish Chandler did the unthinkable.

He simply ran away from second base and squatted down to pick up his wailing daughter and rock her in his arms.

"Hey, Pastor, you still in the game?" somebody called.

"Count me out for now!" he shouted back, then stroked Annie's blond hair, pushing wet strands off her face as she sobbed against his chest.

B.J. watched, deeply touched that a three-year-old could have drawn him away from the competition. Why, if she had even thought to do anything like that to her own father, he'd have called her a wimp.

She watched how tenderly Hamish ministered to his

daughter, and she caught herself juggling both envy and compassion for the beautiful little girl in his arms.

Two women from the bleachers wandered out to the field to check on father and daughter, and Annie lifted herself off her father's chest long enough to show them something on her wrist. One of the women kissed it, and the other patted the little girl's cheek. B.J. suspected they were as interested in the handsome widower father as in his daughter's problem. All three of them walked back to the bleachers, and Hamish sat next to her wheelchair, Annie still in his arms. He twisted Annie around so that she was sitting on his thighs, her back leaning against his chest.

B.J. wondered what her life might have been like if her father had been like Hamish, hugging her when she hurt, turning his back on his all-fired precious competition when she needed him, holding her within his loving protection, cherishing her as if she were the most important person in his world, promising that he would always be there for her.

These little girls might have a happy childhood, B.J. thought, but surely they would grow up soft and puny, crying at the slightest fright, dependent for life on someone stronger and more capable, rejected in the end because they were weak.

There was something about the way Hamish held his daughter, though, that made her ache to lean on him, too.

Annie held out her wrist toward B.J., but abruptly turned away when she looked into B.J.'s face and seemed to remember she didn't like her. "Billy bit me," she said, sniffing, appealing once again to her daddy.

There on her baby skin were two pink half circles of teeth marks. "Bad Billy," B.J. said, suddenly incensed that anyone, even another child, had dared to harm Annie, the epitome of sweet innocence. For a fleeting moment, she wished the wound were her own instead of Annie's. She inhaled sharply at the thought, realizing it had been a flash of protectiveness. "What are you going to do about this?" she demanded of Hamish.

"Talk to his mother," he said, his eyes on the game.

"Aren't you going to get back in the game? Your team needs you." She still couldn't believe how easily he had walked away from the competition. She couldn't seem to stop herself from challenging him.

"Annie needs me."

"You're going to make a sissy of her," she said, but she didn't really believe it. At what price had *she* been denied such tenderness?

He turned his head slowly toward her, and when she looked into his blue eyes, she was astounded to see a profound sadness. "I hope to teach her that love and caring can heal almost anything, and forgiveness costs nothing," he said. "What do you know about love, Brenda Jane?"

She found herself scoffing from lifelong conditioning. Talk of love frightened her. "I'm not a child. And I've always thought love was an overrated emotion." He was right, though. She knew in her heart he was right.

"Have you ever loved anyone?"

"My father, in a way," she said, looking away from him toward the players. His question was causing her throat to constrict, as if another lie would close it off completely.

"Then we'll have to work on that, won't we?" he said, focusing once again on the game.

She felt ashamed and intimidated because he was addressing her inability to understand how he could so easily love and nurture those around him, leaving himself vulnerable to hurt and rejection. She felt she should fight him when what she really wanted to do was throw herself against him as his children did and know he would be there to catch her. And hold her. Any time she needed him. Or wanted him. He was the only person she had ever known who might be able to do that. Be there for her.

It was a terrifying thought. He was a Trojan horse, invading under the guise of being a gift, stealing through her defenses.

She left with Mrs. Billings and the girls shortly before nine, but Hamish had to stay and see that everything was put away, closed and locked up for the night.

At nine-thirty, she was still waiting for him. Some Meeting Night, she thought. Ten minutes of prayer and nearly two hours of play. What kind of Meeting Night was that? She intended to ask him.

Mrs. B had ushered the children up to bed. Emma had hesitated for only a second before she scampered up the stairs, glancing at B.J. as she did so.

"Night, Brenda," the little girl said as she hurried out of sight.

Mrs. B trudged behind them, pulling on the polished wood railing with each step. She threw a weary smile to B.J., then tightened her lips and raised her eyebrows as if to apologize because the children had ignored her.

That was when it finally dawned on B.J. that the girls were avoiding her for "good nights" that probably involved hugs and kisses. She had seen that ritual in other families, children making the rounds of the adults before they went to bed. Delaying the dreaded bedtime, she thought, rather than bestowing affection for a few hours' absence.

She had learned to keep such cynicism to herself, having discovered as a youngster that people were generally sensitive about such family traditions. She felt a twinge of regret, however, that Emma and Annie did not feel an inclination to go through the motions of a bedtime ritual with her. The girls obviously held no affection for her, even vivacious Emma. They might not care for her, but they had a certain sweet air of innocence about them that B.J. found oddly appealing.

Fifteen minutes later, Mrs. B came just far enough down the stairs to peer around the wall at the top of the railing. "I'm sure Pastor will be home shortly to help you up the stairs," she said. "Forgive me, but I have to get up early in the morning."

"Please do get to bed," B.J. agreed. "Sleep well." Polite words, meant for courtesy only. And still, little thing that it was, she truly meant them for Deborah's aunt, who didn't seem to have a dishonest thought in her head.

By ten o'clock, B.J. was beginning to churn with resentment that Hamish had not come home. She thought about the small group of men and women who had clustered around him as most people were leaving, and she realized they were linked by a kind of camaraderie. Probably his cleanup crew. And they had gone out for a drink—coffee most likely, she amended—to laugh and relax together.

She wondered if one of the women in the group had her eye on Hamish. Or did Hamish have his eye on someone? She remembered their short conversation when he said he'd been thinking of marriage. The thought of his sitting somewhere with an attractive woman, someone familiar, someone in tune with church things, pierced her strong defenses and hit upon her vulnerability. She couldn't hope to compete with a whole woman for his attention. She was waiting for him, helpless to get upstairs to bed without his help. And why shouldn't he lose track of time in the company of a woman who had all the qualifications to be a minister's wife?

A little past ten, when he finally sauntered in, she refused to look at him, forcing her eyes to stick to the TV.

"Hi," he said as if it were morning and they were fresh

for a new day. He perched one hip on the arm of the couch alongside her wheelchair. "Uh-oh."

She looked up quickly to see what mishap had brought that response from him. He winced with a half grin.

"I'm in trouble," he said, eyeing her closely. "Sorry I'm so late." He shrugged and sighed in mock chagrin. "The life of a dedicated minister, you know."

Geared up to let him have the full blast of her frustration, she found herself amused by the paradox he presented at that moment. He looked anything but her idea of a dedicated minister. His sweat-stained T-shirt had dried. His khaki shorts were wrinkled. His long, muscular legs lightly furred with pale copper were close enough to touch, and they looked very touchable. His sneakers were grass stained. His bronzed hair lay in chaotic clumps, and she could see the beginning of a light shadow on his face. His laughing blue eyes were focused on her like lights. His body, healthy and hard, beckoned, invited.

She turned away. Amusement faded quickly, driven by a shot of desire so powerful and so unfamiliar she heard herself gasp, felt her muscles tighten. She shut her eyes tight and held her breath to deal with the force that ran rampant through her body. She'd heard of such a thing. She'd never had to deal with it before.

"Brenda? Brenda?" The sound moved from her side to the front of her, his baritone husky, alarmed. She opened her eyes to find him squatting before her, holding on to the arms of her chair. "Are you in pain?"

She might have laughed but for the overwhelming grip of passion she tried to fight. The blue eyes were swallowing her. The straight nose, hard cheekbones and parted lips adorned a face created to entice and seduce. Couldn't he see her own body was drugged with his effect on her?

Shaking her head wildly in response to his question, she once again closed her eyes, but opened them quickly, for closing them only made her more keenly aware of the rich heat liquefying her insides.

Barely aware of her actions, she reached out and placed her hand lightly over his right cheek. She could feel the prickle of a new beard. Moving up, her fingertips invaded the hair over his temple, thick, coarse hair, very masculine, a bit shaggy, needing a trim. And then her hand moved on its own and slid behind his neck, exerting only the slightest pressure to bring his face closer.

She knew his lips would be soft and cool, and they were. She knew they would nibble at hers, and they did. She knew the contact would only heighten the intense longing, and it did.

She didn't know his hands would cup her face, or that his mouth would take over and gently conquer, leaving her helpless and dazed. Nothing that had ever happened to her before had prepared her for Hamish Chandler's sensual power.

Without intent, her good arm slid around his neck, her hand splaying over the muscles in his back, hard, sleek muscles she wanted to feel through his skin, not his shirt. She ran her hand down his shoulder, over the firm mounds of his biceps and up to his neck. Everywhere she found hardness, masculine strength in restraint, channelled into passion and tenderness.

And something else. Definitely something else. She clearly felt his potent need. She felt it in the way his mouth pressed again and again, and the way his hand stroked slowly downward, cupping her ribs, his thumb lightly scraping over her nipple. She felt her body responding to him, welcoming him.

Nothing had ever been like this. She hadn't known anything *could* be like this, totally overpowering, stirring an exquisite spell from which she hoped never to awaken.

It was Hamish who finally broke the kiss. "No," he

whispered, holding her slightly away, his hands still cupping her face. She felt the warm flow of his breath against her upper lip when he'd spoken.

He slowly pushed her against the back of her chair, his palm on the center of her chest. The passion and the need in him were written boldly in his features, and yet he held her away, shaking his head in short motions, as if shedding dust from his hair.

It seemed to take a long time for her senses to return, for her to realize what they had done. No, what *she* had done, reaching out to seduce him like an undisciplined wanton.

Oh, God, what had she done?

As her body slowly cooled, she hung her head in shame, embarrassed to the very core of her being. It was a new thing, feeling passion for a man, and it left her feeling frail, almost ready to shatter. That was when her defenses kicked in, insulating her, giving her tenuous abilities to fight back.

"Nice," she quipped. "Were you pretending I was a real woman?"

"There was no pretending," he whispered. "You're as real as they get."

He stood slowly, looking down at her. She tried to smile at him, as if it had not been a big thing, but she couldn't. Garnering all her resources, she could only watch him fighting off the effects of passion and admire his self-control. Focusing on his face, she squinted to blur her vision because she didn't want to look at his body again, a body she thought might have been created to taunt all the women he didn't want.

He turned and strode away from her, running a hand through his hair and then sliding both hands over his face as if he had just awakened. After a moment, he circled around the coffee table to the back of her chair and pushed her to the staircase.

He stepped in front of her, then dropped to his haunches. "We can't let this happen again, you know," he said softly.

It unnerved her and eroded her defenses that he seemed to be taking more than his share of the blame. She wanted to snap at him, but even her bark was impotent, and she only nodded, whispering, "I know."

"I'm not casual about intimacy anymore, not since Maralynn. She was a..." He inhaled and tried to finish the sentence. "She was..." He couldn't finish it, though.

And she knew why. He was too considerate to tell her he was comparing her with his wife. Only it wasn't a comparison at all. It was a contrast. He looked into her eyes. She wanted to change the subject and didn't know how.

"I was ashamed of the man I once was," he began tentatively. "I wasn't always a pastor, you know. Truth be told, I was the furthest thing from it."

She was speechless at his shocking hint of a dark past.

He absently stirred a fingertip in a stray curl of her hair. "I've learned to push away the guilt I used to feel for the mistakes I made that disrupted other people's lives. I finally realized my past was like a gift, motivating me to reach out to people who don't know we all have choices about how we want to live. It doesn't matter how you start out, or where you come from, or what you've done in the past. We all have choices." He raised himself slowly. "For a few minutes back there, I forgot who I am," he admitted. "I forgot about Maralynn and what I learned from our marriage."

When he didn't speak for several moments, she asked, "What was that?"

"I learned what it's like to love and respect the woman you sleep with, and I'll never again settle for anything less," he said softly.

Like me? she thought, stung by the implication of his words.

He sank to his haunches again and gently gripped her arm on the chair, obviously drawing his own conclusions about her reaction to his response. "That's not a judgment, Brenda, and it doesn't involve anyone but me," he said pointedly. "You deserve so much better."

"You imply that—"

"No, Brenda, it's not what you think." She hadn't heard this voice from him before, the depth of his power, the firm values he embraced. "You're the first woman who has tempted me in many years," he said, rising again. "Now I'm going to pick you up and take you upstairs and set you on the bed. And I think we should both try to forget what just happened here between us."

She closed her eyes while he scooped her into his arms and carried her up the stairs, and she only opened them when he backed into the bedroom and carefully set her on the edge of the bed.

"I hope you can manage," he said quietly. "I'm sorry I was so late tonight. It rarely happens." He backed to the doorway and pulled the door shut. "Goodnight, Brenda," he whispered before the latch clicked.

She struggled out of her clothes and slipped into the nightgown Mrs. B had left on the bed for her. Then she lay down and pulled up the covers Mrs. B had thoughtfully turned down.

Sleep was a long way off. She kept seeing the image of Hamish, handsome, lean and beautiful with eyes as blue as heaven, shaking off the darkness of his past. And there she was, the outsider, the intruder, reminding him that the past was still offering temptation in the form of an unacceptable woman.

Not that she wanted his love, she tried to tell herself. There was no love between them. There was only sexual attraction, which left her aching, restless and angry...and feeling inexorably inadequate.

Chapter Five

B.J.'s avowal to face Hamish with wit and energy the next morning was never put to the test, for Mrs. B, as usual, took over before B.J. was out of bed.

While Annie peeked around the door frame looking ready to bolt at the merest threat, Mrs. B set down a glass of orange juice on the nightstand, then bustled through the closet, pushing hangers, then through the drawers, lifting and prodding and reviewing what she had to work with.

"Bath time," she announced cheerily. "What would you like to wear today? Let's see, Pastor will be here in about forty-five minutes to carry you downstairs, and then we have a half hour until the van."

No longer was B.J.'s first impulse to bark. Now she looked at the solid, joyful form of Deborah's aunt and simply shook her head. Annoyance had given way to amusement after her first day here. Mrs. B was simply homespun, B.J. decided, which was nicely refreshing in her life.

With the help of Mrs. B and one crutch, she managed

to shower and dress. She was sitting on the top step when she heard Hamish come in the back door. She listened to voices below and tried to put herself in gear to face him.

"Medford and Tammy are coming for dinner tonight," Hamish said to Mrs. B. "I hope this is enough notice for you."

"Roast chicken stretches," the woman replied.

Then he appeared on the steps. He stopped abruptly on the landing to look up at her and smile. Her carefully constructed resolve to conquer the effect he had had on her the night before was useless. It didn't help that he seemed to get more handsome every day. Or that his easy smile was like a window to his indestructible joy and gentleness.

He picked her up without effort—as usual—and carried her downstairs, setting her carefully in the wheelchair. Her hand rested on his bicep for support, and she felt its hardness flexing under her palm. He was a powerful man under that coat of gentleness.

When he turned to leave, she stopped him. "What I want to know, Pastor Chandler, is what kind of church is it that has a Meeting Night with ten minutes of prayer and nearly two hours of purely secular play?"

At first he was startled and then he grinned. His answer, when it came, fascinated her in spite of her obvious animosity. She listened with a jutting chin, her left hand gripping her right elbow so that she gave the appearance of having her arms crossed rigidly over her chest. She wanted him to know she had challenged him, not simply asked a question.

With maddening ease, he ignored her attempt to provoke him.

"The purpose of Meeting Night is to bring people and their families together. In the beginning, we met in the all-purpose room and had coffee and visited with one another. But eventually, the quilters broke off, then the children were herded into playrooms, and during the cold weather, we started playing volleyball inside and then softball outside. Sometimes, we play volleyball outside, too.''

He edged toward the old couch and sat on the edge with his elbows on his knees and his hands loosely clasped. Bronze curls draped over his forehead and ears. He needed a haircut.

"Eventually, several people asked if we couldn't start with a short service, something for the families, and, well, things just evolved into what they are today. I guess, if you looked beneath the surface, you'd find there are at least half a dozen support groups meeting while all this is going on. The quilters, for one, and the young mothers in the playrooms, and the people working on crafts, and the cleanup crew, for instance.''

"All those people are in your congregation?" she asked, easing her right arm back to the arm of the wheelchair.

"I think so. But guests are welcome, and we don't keep track of who's there and who isn't," he said. "I've been trying to attract more teens, but maybe we'd be more successful if we planned a Friday night activity just for them. Medford is calling a task-force meeting on Saturday morning to make some recommendations.''

"This isn't a church, it's a social service," she scoffed.

He laughed softly, causing a warm jolt to cross her chest. "Oh, it's a church all right. More than six hundred families are members. We're kind of old-fashioned here, I suspect. Next Saturday afternoon, we're having a potluck picnic with the good old games—you know, egg toss, gunnysack race and relays that include adults and kids together. There's something for all ages, little kids to great-grandparents. You're invited. All the potato salad and nut bread you can eat. And volleyball and Ping-Pong tournaments. How are you at darts?''

It was his easy laughter as much as his handsome face

and athletic body that melted her resistance. "I'm a terror at darts."

"Then you'll have to compete."

"No way."

"Nobody's going to force you to have fun," he said, grinning.

Never in her memory had anyone ever reacted to her the way Hamish Chandler did. She hadn't known there were people like him, people who laughed and smiled and trusted as if life were still contained in the Garden of Eden and gentleness was a manner of living. He was a fool, it was plain to see, a lovable, gorgeous, pious fool. If he hadn't alluded to a dark past, she would call him naive to a fault.

As he left, Mrs. B handed him a bag lunch she had prepared. "Tammy loves roast chicken. It will work out fine," she said as he was passing through the back door. "The usual time?"

"Medford and I will be at the church. When Tammy gets there, we'll be over. About six," he said. "It's about the youth program."

Then he was gone. The house seemed a little stuffier and quieter without him. B.J. could hear the big old clock in the dining room and the clinking of dishes in the sink.

B.J. wheeled herself into the kitchen. Annie sat at the table, her arms folded, her chin resting on a wrist, her big blue eyes following B.J.'s every move, her little mouth in a grim line.

"Medford? Oh, yes, Tammy's husband," B.J. recalled aloud.

Mrs. B murmured absently, digging in the freezer above the refrigerator. "They love my roast chicken. Now where did I put that last one? I know it's in here somewhere."

"What?"

"The frozen chicken."

B.J. held her tongue. Roast chicken was what you ordered from the deli. Maybe it would be interesting to watch Mrs. B actually prepare a chicken from scratch. She'd never seen it done before.

The housekeeper shut the freezer door. "I'll have to check the freezer in the basement," she said. "Stay here, Annie."

But Annie shook her head and struggled to hurry off the chair. She met Mrs. B at the basement door and clutched at her overblouse, her blue eyes pleading. "No," she said, "I go with you."

"You can't come down the stairs, Annie," Mrs. B admonished, turning the child away. "You know that. It's too dangerous."

"I wanna go," Annie insisted, grabbing again at the hem of the older woman's blouse.

"It's too dangerous. You stay here with Brenda. I'll be right back." Mrs. B pulled her little hands loose and held them affectionately. "It will only take me a minute," she reassured her.

Annie's voice rose. "Wanna go!"

Mrs. B looked over at B.J., embarrassed. "She's afraid of strangers," she said, but it was a lame explanation. B.J. already knew the girls were uncomfortable around her since her outburst at the dinner table.

She tried to help anyway. "You can stay with me, Annie," she said, but the little girl merely clutched at Mrs. B's leg and hung on.

"Now, now, Annie," Mrs. B coaxed. "I'll tell you what. How about if we leave Brenda up here?" Annie nodded vigorously. "And you and I go through that door to the basement. You can sit on the top step and watch me while I go get the chicken from the freezer. All right?" Annie hesitated, uncertain. She glanced at B.J. and then back at Mrs. B. "It's the best I can do," Mrs. B warned.

"Shut the door?" Annie asked.

Mrs. B glanced apologetically at B.J. and agreed. "If you'll stay on the top step and not try to follow me down."

Annie reluctantly compromised and the two disappeared behind the basement door. B.J. sat alone, aware of Mrs. B's muted footsteps slowly descending what she imagined were ancient wooden stairs, likely too high and too narrow for safety. She looked around the kitchen again and squinted to make it blurry. She didn't want to think about the beautiful child with the big blue eyes and how much Annie's fear of her hurt.

Somehow, she must reach the child and let her see that she was not a threat. Somehow.

She heard Mrs. B's slow steps plodding up, and when the door opened, she came in nudging Annie ahead of her, both hands supporting frozen poultry.

"When does Emma get home from school?" B.J. asked Annie, who scooted quickly back to her chair, putting the table between them.

Annie eyed her warily as if she didn't hear.

"The bus stops at the end of the driveway at 3:47," Mrs. B answered, peeling the frosty wrapping off the chicken.

B.J. wheeled away to the porch to watch for the van. High on her priority list, she decided, was building trust with Hamish's daughters.

When Emma stepped off the school bus at the end of the driveway, she seemed puzzled to see B.J. waiting for her.

B.J. laughed. "Want a ride to the house?"

Emma's eyes shot wide-open and her jaw dropped. "On that?"

"Hop on my lap, Em, and we'll take a spin," she invited, laughing at Emma's indecision, which lasted all of fifteen seconds. She carefully positioned the girl over her knees. "Here, push this thing," she said to Emma, putting her small fingers on the control.

Emma was enthralled as she experimented, running full tilt and then jerking to a stop, thrusting ahead and then slowing. They finally maneuvered through the gate and up the ramp to the back door. She expected Emma to jump off, but the little girl stayed on. And when they crossed the threshold into the kitchen, Emma was perched like a brassy majorette, arms folded, chin high, one leg crossed over the other.

The first thing B.J. noticed was that Annie was silently astonished and came running toward them, but stopped a few feet away. "Wanna ride, Annie? It's fun," Emma said, hopping down.

Annie's instant reaction was to start forward, but then she looked into B.J.'s face and stopped, shaking her head, pursing her lips. B.J. leaned toward her. "I'd love to give you a ride, Annie," she said softly. Annie's eyes were fraught with conflict, and at one point she sucked at her lower lip, but she didn't move. "Tell you what, Annie. When you want a ride, you let me know, okay? Maybe later?"

Annie looked as if she wanted to nod, but she just skipped away, following Emma into the dining room.

Mending fences was going to take some time, Brenda Jane decided, but she wasn't going to give up on it.

Shortly after six, Hamish came through the back door with the Bantzes. Medford was dark and bony with a black mustache and red shaving blemishes under his chin. When he smiled, he displayed crooked teeth. It was a nervous smile and his Adam's apple bobbed. He did, however, complement Tammy's peaches-and-cream, nice-girl look. She had been a cheerleader, B.J. guessed, and had sung in the church choir, and Medford had been her bookish high school boyfriend who'd never touched her until they were married.

"So you're Brenda," said the Reverend Medford Bantz when they were introduced. "How interesting."

B.J. disliked having everyone hovering above her as she sat in the chair, but she smiled because she had promised Hamish she would not offend his guests.

"What a blessing that Reverend Chandler was able to take you in," Medford said.

B.J. saw Hamish flinch at the inappropriate remark. She cast him a glance as she shook the young minister's hand, letting Hamish know that at least her rudeness was up-front and deliberate, while this man's was masked by his collar. She also let him see that she was holding to her promise.

"My fervent prayers were answered," she murmured, shaking his hand, "when Pastor Chandler rescued me."

She saw the hint of a twitch at Hamish's lips, and then he burst into a devastating smile. Everyone was smiling, but Hamish, she knew, was really laughing.

They sat at the dining-room table, which Mrs. B had set with good china. She noticed that Mrs. B and Hamish had the plates with the chips. Emma chose to sit next to B.J., which made her catch her breath. She resisted an impulse to reach over and hug the girl.

During dinner conversation, B.J. learned that Medford's regular job was as a four-day-a-week chaplain in a chemical dependency treatment center in St. Paul. From what she could gather, he was in charge of one of the Sunday services as part of his duties as assistant pastor at Kolstad Church, in addition to helping out when Hamish went on one of his infrequent vacations. He also took on other various assignments. His latest was organizing a youth program, which both he and Hamish agreed was long overdue. They discussed dates and events, and the people they wanted on the task force. When dinner was over, Mrs. B settled the girls in the living room while Medford and Hamish retreated to Hamish's study.

Tammy immediately began to clear the table and started washing dishes as if she lived there. Obviously, she had done it many times in the three years she and Medford had known Hamish. B.J. was not going to ask, though; she didn't want to hear about the time when this was Hamish's wife's kitchen.

Instead, B.J. listened comfortably to Tammy's chatter while the young woman stacked dishes and waited for Mrs. B to return. She talked about her job as a teacher aide at a nearby elementary school. "It's only ten hours a week, but it helps to pay the bills," she said. "There are so many things I'd like to work on at church, but, well, there just isn't the time, and now I don't have as much energy as I used to."

B.J. felt a surge of envy when Medford came out of the study and headed directly for his wife. She saw his hand linger tenderly as he squeezed his wife's shoulder before he pulled her chair out. She saw Tammy briefly clutch his knuckles and squeeze, and then they exchanged smiles that spoke eloquently of their affection. No one else seemed to notice.

She thought the Reverend Bantz was less than a tenth the man Hamish was, but she felt oddly sad to be on the outside looking in at two people visibly rich with love and respect for each other.

As they were saying good-night at the door sometime later, Tammy started slightly and grinned. Wordlessly, Medford returned the grin and laid his hand over her swelling belly. It was a moment that excluded the rest of the world until Tammy looked at Hamish and murmured, "He moved."

Hamish nodded slightly, his eyes warming as he gazed into Medford's face.

"Incredible. My son," Medford muttered, shaking his head.

"See you Saturday, my friend," Hamish said softly in farewell.

B.J. was disturbed to feel so deeply touched by a condition she had discounted for herself. This new emotion was a source of confusion. Her gaze locked with Hamish's when the couple had departed and he lifted Annie into his arms. She wondered exactly what it was that was passing between them, stirring her insides, leaving her both strangely excited and pensive.

For the first time in her life, B. J. Dolliver felt what it might be like to be a whole, normal woman, and she sensed the fullness of the life women like Tammy Bantz had chosen.

"I've never been around people who laugh as much as you do," she challenged him one day.

"Do you think we're overdoing it? Does it seem unnatural to you?" he questioned, his eyes wide in mock alarm while his lips twitched with suppressed amusement.

"Damn you, Hamish, can't you ever be serious? For a pastor, you seem to hold very little sacred," she snapped.

"Oh, but I do hold quite a few things sacred, dear lady," he said.

It hadn't been a satisfactory answer, of course, insinuating the way it did that she wouldn't understand. But then, rarely were his answers anything but provocative and curiously tantalizing. He still tolerated all manner of insults and mockery from her and still answered with grins and one-liners.

She still waited for him to begin his proselytizing, but she waited in vain, for it never happened.

Life in the Chandler household had offered her new experiences, though. She had rarely in her life been in the company of children for any extended period of time. Emma was lovable, talkative and bubbling with joie de vivre, and the child was rapidly burrowing a place in her heart.

Annie, on the other hand, was still suspicious and refused to communicate with her except to study her intensely from time to time. She and Annie established a pattern of maintaining a wide space between them, although B.J. made repeated efforts to win her trust.

Interesting, she thought, how easy it was to lose her awkwardness with Emma, who would cuddle up to her and enjoy being read to, apparently enraptured with the stories she had heard dozens of times. Sometimes, Annie would listen, too, but always from a safe distance. B.J. experimented with her voice, raising it and lowering it in dialogue, and felt a thrill when Emma giggled.

On many occasions, she wished that she had her cameras to capture their expressions and the beauty of their innocent vitality.

One evening, Hamish met in his study with the chairman of the church's finance committee, a pale, thin, fortyish man with a rigid jaw, squinting eyes and sunken cheeks. Mrs. Billings introduced him as Mr. Edson Forda. As he passed through the living room, he stopped to glare at B.J. "This is the newest addition to your family, Hamish?" he inquired sharply, narrowing his eyes to slits.

"A houseguest," Hamish corrected. "Miss Brenda Jane Dolliver."

"Humph." He looked at Hamish, frowning. "Is she paying rent? Buying her own food?"

For the first time, B.J. saw Hamish squirm. "Uh, could we discuss this in my study?"

"She might as well hear this, Pastor," he said. "If the

congregation is expected to support her, and she isn't even a member."

"I'll pay rent, and the expenses for my care, too," B.J. lashed out.

The little man's head bobbed and his eyes momentarily flared as his gaze flew from Hamish to her and back to Hamish. "How much? Has she paid anything so far?" he demanded of the pastor.

Hamish's eyebrows rose. "I've not expected it, nor would I accept it," he said. "She's a guest of my family. I invited her."

"She's quite attractive. And single." The suggestive tone in his voice chilled B.J. "Doesn't look like a very wholesome situation," he added.

She saw Hamish's face tighten and his eyes harden. There was no amusement in him now, she thought. None at all. "We will discuss this in my study if you please. It's not Miss Dolliver's concern," he said.

"Then we're back to the original question, aren't we?" Mr. Forda reminded him in smug appraisal. He let his gaze wander from one to the other, then continued to address Hamish while he stared at B.J. "Miss Dolliver, a young single woman, living in the home of our widowed minister—"

"That's enough, Edson," Hamish interrupted.

"How much rent would be satisfactory, Mr. Forda?" B.J. snapped.

"It's out of the question. You may deduct what you think fair from my salary," Hamish retorted.

"Hah!" the little man guffawed gleefully.

"In my study, Edson. *Now*," Hamish ordered. B.J. noticed how low and dominating his voice had become, how cold his eyes, how strained his face. It was the first time she had seen him angry like this.

"Perhaps if you let Mrs. Billings go," Mr. Forda said,

bobbing his head gleefully, "and found a wife. You need a wife." It was obvious the man was enjoying Hamish's discomfort.

Hamish moved silently out of the room, his back stiff, his jaw tight.

The little man puffed out his chest and followed. B.J. tried to follow, too, but Hamish stepped in front of the wheelchair before she could enter his study. "Leave this to me, Brenda," he said, and pulled the door shut in front of her.

It might have been unconscionable, but B.J. tried to listen at the door. Her effort was only minimally successful. Then Hamish's voice came to her clearly. "We'll leave it at that for now, then."

She moved away from the door only seconds before it opened. "I'll find my own way out," said Edson Forda, who rapidly came through the door. He hesitated when he saw her, and she saw that his pale face was now pink and his eyes were blazing. Whatever had transpired, he wasn't happy about it.

Hamish followed quickly behind him and caught up with him at the front door barely in time to reach around the little man and open it. "Good evening, Edson," he said. Edson grunted as he passed through. Hamish silently closed the door and turned to face her. "It isn't a problem," he said.

"He's despicable," she told him. "Whoever appointed him to that job?"

"I did."

"Well, can't you unappoint him?"

"I could," he said, striding through the room to return to his study, "but he does a good job of keeping expenses down. He's like an unpaid business manager, even though no one seems to like him."

"He hates you."

"He doesn't approve of me," Hamish corrected her. "He's entitled to disagree. He's still an asset to the congregation."

This time, she followed him into his study. "I have money, Hamish. Let me pay my way here."

"It isn't necessary. I invited you. You're my houseguest."

"Bend your pride," she retorted, her voice harsher than she intended. "I'll feel more comfortable if I can pay my way."

He sighed and sank into his office chair, stretching his long legs to cross at the ankles. "I'm not up to another debate right now," he said. "Maybe we could discuss this some other time."

She was all charged up to argue, to go to the mat with her anger, but the weariness in Hamish's face halted her, whisked away in one swift stroke her eagerness for battle. She lifted her hand from the control before her fingers could propel her chair to him, before she came so close to him she could reach out and cup his beautiful face in her hands.

He wouldn't want that, she reminded herself. He would pull away from her and remind her they weren't to touch. Still, she wanted to wipe the weariness from his face. She wanted to hold him in her arms. She wanted him to lay his cheek against her breast and find comfort, peace and softness.

Instead, she watched from across the room as Hamish leaned forward and pinched the bridge of his nose. "It's getting late. I'll carry you up," he said quietly.

With only a slight hesitation, she turned the chair and rolled it to the foot of the stairs. He leaned down and gathered her carefully into his arms. Before taking a step, he looked down at her and smiled wearily. She draped her good arm over his shoulder and massaged the muscles of his neck with her strong fingers. He let his head fall back slightly and sighed, his eyes closed.

She was giving him pleasure.

He opened his eyes and took the steps slowly. When he reached the bedroom, he set her on the edge of the bed as he did every night, but she continued to massage his neck and shoulders. "Lie down," she said softly. "Let me do this for you."

"I shouldn't," he said, but allowed her to continue rubbing his sore muscles. Usually Mrs. B helped her to bed, but it was late. Everything was set out for her, and Mrs. B was already asleep in her own room.

"Please. There's so little I can do for you," she whispered, pulling him toward her with her good hand until he gave in and sprawled across the bed alongside her.

She maneuvered her leg into a comfortable position and slipped her hand under his collar, massaging the tight cords in his neck, then moving her hand down to his shoulders, rubbing expertly, as she had enjoyed having done to her hundreds of times in the past in training rooms at the tennis clubs where she played.

When her fingers were cramping with the unfamiliar pressure, she simply rubbed her palm over his skin. He was asleep now, breathing deeply, and she wanted to keep him with her where she could touch him. She let her palm wander slowly over his shirt, down the hard corded muscles of his back to his waist, and lower to the belt of his trousers. He was a sexy man, strong and lean, and she liked the feel of him through his clothes.

She knew she should wake him, knew he would be horrified that he had fallen asleep on her bed. She definitely intended to wake him in just a few more minutes. Touching the side of his face, she felt the short stubble of beard, then she turned and lay down on her back alongside him to watch him sleep, to study the features that formed the most beautiful masculine face she'd ever seen.

She looked at copper eyelashes lying against high, tanned cheeks, a long, straight nose, perfectly symmetrical, perfectly shaped, and the small sculptured valley from the middle of his nose to his upper lip, which curled outward slightly. His lips were barely parted, revealing tips of his even white teeth.

She rolled toward him and brought her face next to his so that each puff of his breath floated over her face. And then she leaned closer and barely touched his lips with hers, just brushed them with hers, ever so lightly.

She stopped when he caught his breath for a second, then she watched his tongue dart out and lick his upper lip while he slept. His head jerked back and he rolled away slightly, but was still facing her. She moved closer into the nest of his arms, raising her head to rest it on one hard bicep and feeling the other drape over her back.

Hot liquid seeped low in her belly, and she felt a compulsive yearning to be even closer, to touch the full length of him with her body, to lie next to him, to be in his arms for a longer time, to feel him pressed still closer, to be full of him.

She felt his hand tighten against her back, pulling her more snugly against him. She felt the quickening of his body, the hardening and swelling. And then she felt his breathing change and his hips undulate slowly against her, bringing another, more intense rush of heat and a need that overwhelmed her good intentions.

She lifted her knee over his hip to give him better access, then lost her head when he shifted slowly, with tender, instinctive passion against the most sensitive part of her. Moving her lips to his, she touched his mouth lightly until he nibbled at her and finally kissed her fully, his tongue invading and searching, caressing, joining.

As his movements became less tender and more demanding, she felt him awaken, and she held him to her. "Oh, Brenda, Brenda," he groaned, and then he slid over her, taking her breath away with his sweet, possessive loving and a passion she had never known before. His large, full length pressed her into the mattress as he lay between her legs.

She wanted him desperately with every molecule in her trembling body.

But he pulled his lips away and stopped the seductive action of his hips. He leaned his forehead against hers while he held himself upon his elbows. His breathing was rapid and ragged, fanning her face. "Help me to stop," he whispered, his voice heavy with anguish. "Don't let me—"

She placed her index finger over his lips. "I don't want you to stop, Hamish," she whispered back to him.

His body stiffened as he inhaled deeply and pushed himself onto his knees. He gazed down at her, his eyes smoldering with desire, and then he lowered his head until his lips were against her right breast. He rubbed his lips over the fabric of her blouse where it covered her hard nipples, then he pushed himself backward so that he sat on his heels between her legs.

He was hugely beautiful, even fully dressed, poised like a potent lover ready to mount. But he had spurned her before. And B.J. could see that his damnable conscience was winning, tearing him away from her as painfully as if he was of her very flesh.

He rested his big, gentle hands, fingers splayed, firmly on her thighs. For a moment, she thought he would succumb to her invitation and to the desire that was written as visible as block letters in his eyes as his thumbs began to graze over the sensitive area between her thighs.

She sensed he was a highly skilled lover. She could feel it in his hands, see it in his eyes as he fought within himself. He was undoubtedly a very sensual man who knew how to pleasure a woman. He was smooth and artful. She remembered the hints he'd dropped about being a bad boy in earlier days, and about his learning the importance of love and respect in a sexual relationship.

In the next second, he was off the bed, pacing away from her, combing fingers through his hair, breathing deeply. He turned finally and stood at the foot of the bed, looking as though he had just fought a painful battle, his arms spread, the tall bedposts taking his weight with a large hand on each. His lips were moving as though he was trying to form the words to speak, but he eventually just shook his head and pressed his eyes closed.

Was he remembering his wife?

Or was he even now including B.J. in the ranks of the women he was ashamed to remember?

She rolled to her right side and curled up in a ball, holding her right elbow to keep her arms against her stomach. She couldn't face him. For the first time in her life, she had truly, deeply, wanted a man to make love to her and had offered herself to him without conditions.

She had made a fool of herself. He had told her outright that he would not settle for less than being in love with the woman he took to his bed. It was a matter of principle with him.

And Hamish Chandler, she had learned, was a highly principled man.

She wanted to hide from him, for he had just let her

know that she was less than acceptable. It mattered little how much she aroused him. She was less than what he wanted.

She wasn't good enough.

Again.

Chapter Six

B.J. lay in bed, watching the sun blast its first rays over the horizon. She struggled to sit, exercising the fingers on her right hand as she did first thing every morning. She lifted and lowered and bent her right arm, massaged the toes, calf and thigh of her right leg, then she stood on the floor next to the bed, her weight on her left.

Hamish was going to make her leave. She just knew it. But she wasn't going to allow it.

Rejection was like the opening salvo from an enemy army. When the hurt was overrun by anger, she fought back, highly motivated to win, armed to the teeth with resolve and a backbone like concrete.

It had always worked for her, ever since the first time her father shunned her because she wasn't a boy, and girls, he said, could never throw a baseball like a boy. She was hopeless, he'd said. She threw a baseball like a *girl*.

She was nine years old and she'd watched him walk away from her disappointed and angry. Well, she couldn't become a boy, but she could certainly learn to throw a ball like one if that was what he wanted. She'd wiped away the tears and hung around his franchise in the Chicago suburb until a player from a farm team came to see her father. She'd tugged at his sleeve, then took her stance in front of him and asked if he would teach her how to throw a ball like a boy.

His name was Charlie, and he'd openly shoplifted a new ball from her father's stock and taken her out to the parking lot where he taught her how to throw it. Her arm had ached for two days, but when he came back for another lesson, he said she'd gotten the hang of it.

The next day when her father was behind the counter harassing the store manager, she'd stood in the doorway of the store and yelled to him, "Hey, Pat, *catch!*"

He had, and he'd thrown the ball back to her, risking a broken window. Then he had picked her up and swung her around and told her she was the greatest.

The lesson was simple.

Life was one battle after another. The secret was never to accept defeat, never to surrender. The key was always to be strong.

Deep inside, she knew she wasn't good enough to be the child her father wanted, but she had fought to keep him from knowing it. She had fought every day to impress him. She still fought every day for whatever it was she wanted. It was a way of life.

She had fought her editors for the assignments she wanted. She had fought art directors to insure the best placements for her photos. She had fought coaches in order to be the best she could be at tennis.

If it was worth having, it was worth fighting for.

She stood in silence and looked at the distance between her feet and the door. Sometimes, when she could stand alone, she wished for just five minutes to be free from infirmity, to take a few steps, to remember what it was like to walk, one foot in front of the other, both legs working normally. Just five minutes' worth.

Using the strength of her left leg, she lowered herself to the carpet and dragged her body to the bathroom, then back again to her closet, where she crawled up the dresser in order to stand and reach her clothes. Dressing was clumsy and frustrating, and usually Mrs. Billings helped.

This morning, though, she had felt a resurgence of motivation. When she was dressed, before anyone else was up, she dragged herself along the floor to the top of the stairs and then edged to the left so that she could reach up and grasp the railing.

She had thought of it long and hard during the night, planning how she would accomplish staying in this house until she was well enough to leave. Sitting at the top of the stairs with one useless leg and one nearly useless arm, B.J. looked at the frightening view down the steps. If she slipped, if she lost her grip, if she fell… But she wouldn't. She was capable of being deliberate and cautious, taking each step as a separate project.

It seemed to take forever, and by the time she reached the landing, she was drained and perspiring. She lay on her back with her feet on the next step for what seemed a long time, recovering her strength. The sleepless night she'd had certainly did not help.

When her feet were on the floor, she wiped the sweat from her face and pulled herself to a standing position. Her wheelchair sat to the side of the newel post. She shifted and pulled against the post to position herself, then fell backward into the chair. If the house had not been eerily silent, she'd have cheered aloud. It was a delicious victory.

Once in the kitchen, she started the coffee and made herself toast. The toast was history and the cup of coffee half-gone when Hamish plodded out of his study, barefoot, wrapped in a loosely tied bathrobe, his hair tousled and his eyes squinting.

He blinked several times when he saw her. "How did you get down here?"

"Magic carpet," she said, sipping her coffee, avoiding his chest where it was exposed.

He studied her face. "How?"

She glanced at his intent blue eyes, then looked away. Her voice was scratchy when she spoke again. "The pertinent question, Hamish, is why. Ask me why."

"Why, then?" He pulled out a chair and sank into it, eyeing her suspiciously, his elbows on the table. His thick bronze hair stood out in ten directions.

She cleared her throat and tried not to look at him. She caught his scent and felt his warmth. This was what it would be like to wake up with him, she thought. "Because of last night. Because of what happened."

He rubbed his eyes and face with his hands, then he studied her with a more alert expression. "I'm sorry, Brenda. Please accept my apology for that." She didn't miss the slight edge in his voice.

"But, Hamish, you have nothing to apologize for. It was all my fault," she told him, following her meticulously rehearsed script, knowing her voice was sounding forced. "I didn't mean to take advantage of you while you slept. Really, it was not premeditated. I simply lost my good sense, and then, well, things just got out of hand. I take full responsibility, Hamish, for, um, accidentally seducing you." She watched the emotions play over his face—disbelief, confusion, frustration. "It won't happen again," she promised, gripping his forearm as if she didn't have his full attention. "It won't happen again." Was she sounding annoyed, she wondered, or strident?

The tightening of his lips and the hardness in his eyes

told her that her worst fears were being realized. "No, it certainly won't," he said.

"Hamish," she cried, "don't even think it. You can't send me away."

"I can't let you stay here. You're not safe with me, Brenda," he said softly, clasping his big warm hand over her knuckles. There was compassion in his eyes. It angered her.

"That's ridiculous. How can you even consider it?" she demanded. She was desperate to win this essential round, an effort that was appearing to be despairingly hopeless. "Why now, when I've learned to navigate the stairs and you won't have to carry me anymore? You won't ever have to touch me again. Everything is different now. Surely you can see that, Hamish? Surely you're not going to throw me out when I'm making progress."

Hoping the harsh rise in her voice would persuade him, she watched the slight twitch in his jaw muscle as he concentrated, his indecision obvious.

"It's working," she insisted, her anger releasing a strident tone she was unable to control. "My being here is making me better. Surely you can see that."

He leaned away from her. "We'll see about that," he said. "I'm planning to talk to Dr. Wahler today."

Fighting the chaos of conflicting emotions, she slumped in her chair and covered her eyes with her left hand. "Spare me the threats, Hamish," she choked. "Just look at me. I made it downstairs on my own. And I can make it back up by myself, too."

When she looked up, his face was suddenly unreadable, and for the first time she felt his deep inner strength as a formidable power.

Attack had always been her natural reaction to fear. She had found it an intimidating force that got her her way. Yet, she should know by now that Hamish had a rare emotional maturity, and contrived drama would gain her nothing with him.

Her heart beat faster when she realized what she was doing. It wasn't just *winning*. This time, it was something more, something necessary for breathing, existing.

He pushed the chair back, scraping it along the old flooring. "We'll see," he said, and headed for the shower in the upstairs bathroom.

B.J. sat in bereft silence. Had he already decided to send her away? Without considering why the thought terrified her, she knew she had to persuade him to let her stay.

Mrs. Billings was loudly vocal in her delight over B.J.'s early-morning achievement on the stairs, and Emma was insistent that B.J. demonstrate her new prowess. "Later," she told the six-year-old. "Tonight, when it's time to go to bed. I'll go early, at the same time you do, just so I can show you how it's done." She wondered just how difficult and frightening the ordeal was going to be.

At breakfast, she listened attentively to Hamish telling Mrs. Billings about his schedule for the day. Normally, she paid little attention. She watched him lift each child into his arms and have a private conversation while he lovingly ran his gentle hands over their hair and lightly pinched their cheeks. Then he kissed them goodbye, advised them to take good care of Mrs. Billings and Brenda Jane and headed in long strides down the driveway and across the road.

When the hands of the clock said it was nearly ten, she told Mrs. Billings she wanted to venture over to the church. She knew Hamish would be in a meeting, but she wanted to test her courage by wheeling to the church herself. Mrs. Billings didn't like the idea, but she didn't try to stop her, and B.J. quickly made use of the ramp Hamish had installed over the back steps to get herself outside before Mrs. Billings changed her mind.

For a minute, she felt frightened to be alone outside, to be crossing a road on her own for the first time since her accident. As she traveled down the church road, she heard the whisper of needles on the towering pines, the faint rustle of dead leaves on branches and the low whine of the chair motor.

She laughed at herself for feeling as though she was on an adventure, but that indeed was what it was. She inhaled the pungent smell of damp, cold wood and noted the shriveled ferns along the gravel road. She sucked in her breath at the sight of the imposing brick edifice that was Hamish's church. Still, she sensed how solid it was. She had some trouble with the door, but she managed it finally, and moved into the narthex, stopping at the open double doors to the nave.

Hamish was there, kneeling on the steps of the altar, his elbows on the top of the rail, his head bowed. Her heart tumbled at the sight of him, of this man who held her immediate future in his hands, of the devout pastor whose love for his children was as deep and profound as his spiritual beliefs.

She couldn't imagine her father praying. There were few men she knew who had the courage to be seen doing it. Hamish Chandler had more depth and courage and honesty than any man she had ever known, and it was all blended with his humility and his joy. It was in these moments, watching him pray at the silent altar of his church that she realized she admired him and trusted him in a way she had never experienced with anyone before.

It startled her to realize how much this simple man in this simple rural-suburban community had come to mean to her.

He backed down the two steps and stood in silence for a few moments before he turned to leave. As he walked to the side door, he looked out over the church, from the choir loft to the windows, then stopped abruptly when he saw her. She fought the tears that began to sting her eyes. She fought them back because they were a sign of weakness and she'd never wanted to be weak.

He changed his direction and strode toward her, large and masculine and graceful.

He was wearing his collar.

It did something to her, that collar, stiff and white, emerging from the chocolate brown fabric, framed by a tweed blazer. It was his work uniform, just as a businessman wears a suit, a mechanic his coveralls.

She met him partway up the aisle. When he was a dozen feet from her, she stopped, kicked the wheelchair's footrests aside and stood. As he stopped before her and whispered her name, she trembled and fell to her knees. She tried to stand, tried to speak, but lost her fight to resist the burning tears.

"No...Brenda, no." His words were softly spoken, and she felt him trying to get a grip under her arms to lift her up.

When he'd nearly succeeded, she sat back on her heels and leaned forward, covering her face with her left hand. He stepped back as she huddled in the aisle. She wasn't aware that he squatted before her until he lifted her so that she straightened on her knees. She felt a sharp pain shoot from her right knee to her injured pelvis, but ignored it.

"Brenda," he pleaded raggedly, holding her up before him, "what is it?"

Her head was bowed as she tried to stop the tears, but it was too late, for she was sobbing out of control. He lifted her yet again, and when she was standing on her good leg, he gathered her in his arms and held her against his chest.

"Don't...send m-me...away," she managed to say.

"I can't send you away," he said softly, bending to

murmur into her hair. "I know I should, but I can't. I don't
know why you're in my life, but there must be some purpose other than to tempt and torment me. Or maybe you're
here just to remind me I'm only a man, with all the flaws
and deficiencies one might expect. Or to tell me it's time
for me to take another wife. I've already decided, Brenda
Jane, that when you're mended enough to be on your own,
my first order of business will be to start looking for a
wife. I'm not sure how to go about it exactly, but I know
a lot of people who will have advice for me on the matter.
I won't send you away. I'm going to take good care of
you until you've recuperated enough to take care of yourself. I can't explain what I'm feeling, except to say that
this feels right."

His words were spoken softly and they touched her like
a balm on her soul and a twist on her heart. So appalled
was she at her loss of control that she didn't give a thought
to why she reacted as she did, or why he both soothed and
disturbed her with his passionate discourse.

When her sobbing finally subsided into occasional hic-
cups and he handed her his threadbare, neatly folded handkerchief, she was depleted of energy and thought.

For the first time in her life, she felt as though she had
surrendered.

Still, she didn't feel that she had exactly lost anything.

None of it made sense.

"Thank you," she sniffed, covering her face with the
handkerchief, wetting it thoroughly.

Hamish grasped her by the shoulders, holding her upright. She couldn't look at him. "Are you all right? I have
a meeting now with Mrs. Deaton that I must get to. Or
rather, I *had* a meeting with Mrs. Deaton about ten minutes
ago."

"You still do, Pastor," a strident voice called from the
vestibule. "What's this nonsense?"

B.J. heard the muted thunk of heavy heels on the rubber mat of the center aisle as Mrs. Deaton approached them. B.J. looked up at Hamish in apology and noticed his brown shirt stained with splashes of her tears.

"Hello, Mrs. Deaton," Hamish greeted as she approached him from behind.

B.J. saw the woman step around him and glare at her with sharp eyes encased in fine wrinkles and a hint of eye shadow. She was a woman in her sixties at least, well dressed in a conservative suit of navy blue pinstripes. She clutched a large handbag protectively to her stomach as though it contained gold.

Hamish reached up and used his thumb to rub away an errant tear, then turned and smiled at Mrs. Deaton. "This is my houseguest, Brenda Jane Dolliver. Mrs. Deaton is head of the building-and-grounds task force and the long-range planning committee, two very important posts."

"So this is the celebrity," Mrs. Deaton declared. Her voice was harsh and commanding. "Not in the best of shape, I see."

"Bad day. But she's making excellent progress in her recuperation. She's standing. That's something," Hamish said, smiling at B.J. in a way that set her heart racing.

"With a great deal of help, I see," Mrs. Deaton replied. Her penetrating gaze zeroed in on the damp patches on his shirt.

"Brenda needed a shoulder," he said as if she wasn't capable of answering for herself.

But it was one of the rare occasions in her life when B. J. Dolliver couldn't think of a thing to say.

"Doesn't look good, Hamish, pretty young thing hanging on to you like that," Mrs. Deaton said. "Good thing it's me here instead of old Edson Forda."

B.J. felt herself blush when Hamish smiled and said,

"He would make something mountainous of it, wouldn't he?"

"Well, he isn't the only one crowing about appearances," Mrs. Deaton snapped. "I think he sees Ms. Dolliver as just another obstacle to your finding a suitable wife."

"Is that right?" Hamish scoffed playfully.

But Mrs. Deaton was eyeing B.J. sharply, pausing at the jagged little scar still visible on her cheek. It was probably bright pink about now with all her makeup cried away, she thought. Even Mrs. Deaton could see she wasn't wife material.

"That's *wrong!*" B.J. choked with flashing belligerence. "Pastor is looking for a wife. Why, we spoke of it just the other day." *We're going to find him one with a whole face, and legs and arms that work,* she added silently.

Mrs. Deaton quirked her eyebrows. "I see," she returned knowingly, then winked at B.J. as if they shared a secret. Or had she just imagined it? "I'm waiting in your office. Don't be long," she ordered Hamish.

"She's really a good person under all that crust," he whispered, grinning.

"You'd better go," she replied, twisting to see how far she was from her chair.

"Not yet. Not until you're all right. She'll understand," he said.

"I'm fine now, really. Thanks for the shoulder," she told him with more verve than she felt. "Will you pull my chair closer please?"

"Everything's going to work out, Brenda. We'll make it work. You'll be walking on crutches when you leave here," he said, ignoring her request. "And this," he said softly, running a thumb over her fading scar. "I forget about it until someone else points it out. I think it adds character."

"Yes, facial scars can be quite glamorous in a dark sort of way," she agreed, closing her eyes. "Unless you're the one being stared at."

He pulled her against his chest again. She felt the rough tweed of his jacket against her cheek and heard the thumping of his heart behind his ribs. "If you want to wait, I can walk you home when Mrs. Deaton leaves. I worry about you crossing the road alone."

"I can make it. I have to get used to taking care of myself again."

"Not yet, Brenda Jane," he said, hugging her close. "Give it time."

She would have made it, but Tammy came in before she reached the outside door. "Why, Brenda, are you all right?" She was bending over her chair before B.J. could speak. Her warmth was comforting.

"Yes, I'm fine," she said.

"There's usually a pot of coffee on in the kitchen this time of day. Won't you join me?" B.J. shook her head, but before she could get any words out, Tammy pleaded with a sweet open smile, "Please?"

So she went to the kitchen and sat at a table with Tammy while people wandered in and out. "What are all these people doing here?" she asked.

"That man who just wandered through is a retired sheet-metal contractor who is checking the heating system before winter sets in," Tammy said. "And Kathleen Peterson, the woman who helped herself to a cup of coffee and walked away with it just lost her husband, so we've given her a job to make up a mailing list of teens."

"Oh, yes, I remember now," B.J. declared. "Your husband is involved in setting up a task force to organize a youth program, isn't he?"

Tammy's face brightened. "Why, yes!"

"It sounds as if he has quite a hectic schedule."

"Unfortunately, his regular job takes up a great deal of time. This is where he would most like to be, however. We're just waiting for our own church."

"Do you think you'll take over this congregation?" B.J. asked, suddenly seeing the Bantzes as a threat to Hamish's future.

"Oh, probably not," Tammy said. "At first, we thought that's what would happen. The elders at headquarters, and the people in this church...well, marriage is a very important status for their pastors. And when Maralynn became so ill, they could see Hamish needed help, and they, well, I kind of think they expected him to leave. Or something. I don't know. It was all so vague at the time. We jumped on the assignment thinking we were going to get our own congregation, but things haven't worked out that way."

B.J.'s interest was stirred. Was Hamish's job in trouble after all? "So, it's really important that Hamish find a wife, then?"

"Oh, yes. But I can see why it's difficult for him," Tammy remarked, sipping her coffee. "Maralynn was so very perfect. She taught me so much about being a pastor's wife."

"Perfect?" B.J. choked.

"Just about. Even when she was so sick and we all knew she wasn't going to make it, she still supported him and took care of her babies and was so patient with people," Tammy praised. "She was a very gentle woman, a perfect pastor's wife. Quiet but friendly. An excellent cook. Always willing to help out when an extra hand was needed."

"You knew her well?"

"Oh, yes, we got to be good friends. Kindred spirits, I guess. I still miss her. She would be so happy for us," she added, patting her swollen belly.

B.J. felt a sharp, piercing pain streak through her chest.

"Of course," Tammy continued, smiling at something unseen, "she was a very serious person. Laughter made her uncomfortable."

"It did?"

"Oh, yes, the one thing she didn't like was Hamish's boisterousness. And she wanted her girls to be serious." She leaned over the table and giggled. "I think she failed with Emma, don't you? And I'm really glad for Emma."

"Yes," B.J. said, feeling her breath coming raggedly from her lungs. "She's a delight. Like her father."

"Well, I better get to work. Mickey Kostavich is always in charge of the Christmas pageant, and her mother has had a stroke. She may not be able to give it her full attention this year," Tammy said, sipping the last drop from her cup.

"Christmas pageant? It's only the end of October."

"The Christmas pageant is on our minds all year long, Brenda," she said, pushing herself up from the table. "We have a lot of preparations to do around the church. Pastor encourages it. He encourages anything that brings families together. My Medford does, too, although he can't be around to participate as much as he would like."

"Do you think…do you ever wonder…what would happen if Hamish didn't marry again soon?" The question jumped out of her in staggered breaths.

"Oh, he will. He knows it's way past time for him," Tammy said confidently.

Maybe Tammy wasn't thinking about her husband taking over Hamish's congregation, B.J. thought as she watched Tammy walking away, but she wondered if Hamish was in danger of losing his church all the same.

And all because the congregation wanted him to marry again.

When B.J. rode her chair back to the house, she felt for the first time the swift, penetrating cold of late fall. The leaves were yellow and dried, scattered on the ground and crunchy under her wheels.

She felt curiously vulnerable when she wheeled up the ramp onto the porch and then into the kitchen. It was as if she was seeing the house for the first time, as if everything had been tilted slightly off center, and now it was straightened. Once inside, she scanned the big old kitchen and felt its sprawling warmth, rough but comforting, like tweed against her cheek.

"What are you doing?" she asked Mrs. B.

"Making lunch. Chicken salad sandwiches and vegetable soup."

B.J. looked closely as the older woman spread chicken salad thickly on bread and added a leaf of lettuce before covering it with another piece of bread. "I could probably help with that," B.J. said. "If you want me to."

Mrs. Billings stepped aside and stared at her, then smiled. "Yes, that would be nice," she said. "I'll move it to the table. It will be easier for you to reach."

Whatever possessed her to make the offer escaped her, but when she looked at the pile of sandwiches on the serving plate, she believed it was a need to be a part of this family, to be more than an idle visitor everyone stepped around and helped because she was temporarily disabled. She felt an odd need to be accepted, to be liked. So she spent more time with the little Chandler girls, although Annie usually kept Emma between them. She read to them, joined in their games, ironed doll clothes and, three days later, shared their excitement over new kittens.

"I saw kitty and she's skinny again!"

It was Emma racing through the back door, her eyes as big as tree knots. Annie followed behind, grinning, her blue eyes dancing, her head nodding in agreement, as if Emma's words spoke for both of them.

"Well, did you follow her to see where the babies are?" Mrs. Billings asked.

Emma halted abruptly. Her chin dropped as her mouth formed an O. "Oh, no," she wailed. "I don't know where they are."

"Well, sometimes momma cats hide their babies. If you want to find them, you follow the cat," Mrs. Billings said gently, patting Emma's cheek.

Emma turned to her little sister, whose expression changed to match that of her older sister, and the two raced outside again.

"I think I'll go look, too," B.J. said. She wheeled alongside Mrs. Billings, then stopped, looking down at her right hand on the arm of the chair. "Bye," she said, smiling, and lifted her hand and forearm a few inches, wiggling her fingers.

Mrs. Billings laughed. "It's getting better all the time," she said.

It was a good day. B.J. wheeled quickly down the ramp and into the backyard, following the shouts of the girls. Earlier, she had made arrangements to continue with therapy three times a week in a rehab center in White Bear Lake, just a few miles away.

She'd also decided to buy a car. And she had sent the first of her monthly "rent" checks to the church treasurer with a note explaining that Hamish was not to be bothered with the matter. If there was a problem, Mr. Forda was to get in touch with her personally.

Hamish had been friendly and warm, but he had not come within touching distance since the emotional confrontation in the church. When she saw him come home in the evenings, she felt an ache deep inside, as if she had lost a part of herself. She didn't understand it.

Emma's squeals drew her attention to the garage shed, and she followed with some difficulty through the door, thankful that it was on the same level as the ground. Inside, the girls were crawling gingerly up a narrow staircase that was little more than a rough ladder. The steps were only about a foot and a half wide, and each was only about three inches deep, open at the back, a sizable space from one step to the next.

B.J. held her breath while the girls made their way up the stairs, but realized they had probably done it dozens of times, for they were cautious and slow about it. They looked sure of themselves and seemed in no danger of falling. She eyed the staircase thoughtfully, planning how she might raise herself up to the loft above where she could hear the little girls cooing and squealing and talking baby talk to the "babies."

"Hey, Emma! Annie!" she called. "I want to see, too."

Emma's head protruded over the edge. "Want me to bring one down?"

"How many are there?"

"Lots."

"I want to come up. Come and help me to the steps," she ordered, anxious suddenly to see what the fuss was about.

Emma slowly worked her way down the steps backward and gave B.J. a hand to grip. B.J. pulled herself to sit sideways on the step, her left cheek barely finding purchase on the narrow step, her left arm wrapped around the step above. Emma tried to help her up each step, and they giggled all the way, one careful step at a time. And she had thought the stairs in the house were difficult!

She dragged herself across the straw on the floor to the

cat's litter, nestled in loose hay on a ragged, dirty dish towel. It was quite a spectacle all right. Tiny, wiggling balls of fur with eyes sealed shut nursed frantically. There were six of them, mostly black and white, one a silver gray.

B.J. found herself as enthralled as the children and wondered how she had missed this experience in her childhood.

Emma left once to tell Mrs. Billings where they were. She returned to find that the mother cat had left the nest for a while, and the three of them petted the babies away from her watchful eye.

It was only when Hamish came home for dinner and the girls heard his voice that they were motivated to abandon their sport. They scrambled down the steps to greet their father. B.J. was left to drag herself to the rough stairs. She heard their squeals as they headed for the house, knowing Hamish had picked them up, one in each arm, to carry them into the house as he always did. She felt abandoned and yet was grateful he was not there to see her clumsy efforts to get down.

As she tried to place her hip on a narrow step, she heard the back door slam and heavy sprinting down the ramp. He was coming back for her! When she looked up and saw him flying through the side door, she let go of the two by four she'd been holding on to to grasp the step under her ribs. Maybe it was the distraction, or maybe it was her body tensing at the sight of him, but her hip slipped from its perch and her hand failed to catch the top step. She bent her knee to catch herself, but it only threw her weight forward, and when she straightened it, she felt herself falling over the open edge of the stairs.

Hamish was there to catch her, but it was a haphazard catch, for he barely reached her in time, and they both went sprawling on the dirty, cracked concrete. When they came to a stop in their tumble, she was lying across his chest. She looked into his face. "Are you hurt?" she asked, touching his face.

Anger flared in his eyes. "Don't you ever do that again!" He lifted his head and then pushed her carefully off his chest so that he could sit up. He rubbed absently at the hay and dirt on her clothes and frowned at her. "Where's your sense, woman?"

By then, the girls were coming through the door. "Did you fall?" Emma asked.

"I got here just in time," he answered. "Well, almost in time."

"Don't be mad, Daddy. We helped her up the stairs," Emma said, picking at hay on the back of B.J.'s shirt. "We forgot you," she confessed sheepishly. "Daddy came home and we forgot you couldn't just walk down the steps."

B.J. looked at Hamish and Emma squatting on the filthy floor, casually picking debris off her shirt, and she burst into laughter. "I'm perfectly all right," she told them. She turned to get Annie's attention, then winked at her. "Your daddy rescued me. And then he hollered at me. And now everything is all right again, except here we are, all of us getting dirty!"

A slow grin cut the frown from Hamish's face as he pushed himself upright and held a hand out to her.

"We both look like we've been rolling in the hay," she declared when he scooped her into his arms and carried her to the wheelchair. "Hey, don't set me in that thing. It will get all dirty!" She heard Emma giggling. "You'll just have to carry me into the house," she said. "Won't he?" She turned to the girls for support.

"Brenda gets a turn!" Emma cried, reaching for Annie's hand. Even Mrs. Billings was laughing from the doorway.

Brenda Jane had never felt quite so happy.

For the first time, it didn't seem the most important thing to get her old life back.

Chapter Seven

"Yes, Eileen. Yes, I'll see what I can do. He's where? Grant's Cage? I'll talk to him. Don't worry. I'll call as soon as I know anything."

Hamish hung up the telephone and turned to exit his study, realizing suddenly that he should have shut the door for that conversation. Too late. Once he had heard the desperate voice of Neil Haraldson's wife, he had forgotten about who might be listening.

He returned to the table casually, pushing his chair in, ignoring his unfinished dinner. His eyes met those of Brenda across the table, and she was glaring with anger and fear. Fear for him? He smiled weakly, recognizing that she had overheard his conversation and knew Grant's Cage for what it was—one of the roughest bars in the roughest neighborhood in the Twin Cities.

He searched her face for understanding and found none. "I have an emergency to take care of," he announced to his family.

He watched her shake her head slowly from side to side,

her eyes narrowing in accusation. At least, he thought, she didn't blurt it out in front of Mrs. Billings and the children. But he could see he was going to have some explaining to do.

It should have been a nuisance, explaining himself. He rather liked Brenda's concern for him, the way she watched him and understood his moods, slicing through his murky thoughts with ruthless honesty and blunt epithets. He liked the passion she brought to everything she said and did.

"I have to leave. I might be late," he told his family. He leaned over and pecked each daughter on the cheek. "If you're asleep when I get home, I'll come in and kiss you good-night," he promised.

"I don't like when you go out at night," Emma said, pouting.

"I know, sweetheart," he said, touching her tangled brown hair. "I don't like it, either. Don't anyone wait up for me," he added with a grin, but when he turned back to the table, Brenda was right behind him in the wheelchair. "Where are you going?" he asked.

"I'm seeing you to the car," she snapped.

He knew better than to protest when he saw the look on her face, so he let her follow him. Outside, as he expected, she started in on him.

"Don't do it, Hamish. That's the worst neighborhood, absolutely the worst. Don't you read the papers? Two people were stabbed on that street last month. One of them died." She grabbed his sleeve and hung on. "Don't go. Send someone else."

"It's a friend in trouble, Brenda," he told her as gently as he could. "And I don't have time right now. I'll talk to you about it later. Don't worry. I'll be all right."

"You always say that," she retorted. "You don't know how bad it is!"

He looked down at her left hand, her knuckles white from gripping the fabric of his jacket. "I know exactly how bad it is and I can handle myself. Trust me," he asked of her.

"Please, Hamish," she pleaded.

"I'll be all right. I know what I'm doing," he explained, knowing that his reassurances wouldn't be enough for her, that she didn't trust him to know about life on the rough side.

"At least take someone else with you. Like Burton Kostavich or Les Johnson." Her grip tightened, and he felt her twisting the fabric near his wrist. He was impressed that she remembered the names of the two burly men who showed up for Meeting Night on Wednesdays.

"You'll just have to trust me in this," he told her, prying her fingers loose. When he was free of her, he stepped quickly to the side out of her reach and strode to his car. Over the car roof, he admitted, "I'm familiar with the place. I've had lots of experience handling myself there."

He slipped into the car and slammed the door before she could get a word out. He could see that she was still sitting by the driveway when he pulled away and headed down the highway toward the city. Well, he had warned her before that his earlier years had been less than wholesome.

Maybe it was time to tell her the whole story.

It had only been about six weeks since he brought her home, but it seemed as though she had always been there—a cross to bear, so to speak, and a joy more and more of the time. A temptation. An entertaining companion. A pain in the backside. Someone he looked forward to seeing at the end of each day. The one thing she did better than anyone was add color and texture to his life. There was no doubt about that.

And it made him realize how much he missed having a life mate.

Although he appreciated her concern for his well-being, he himself was disturbed by his mission tonight. He hoped she would trust him to know his way around a place like Grant's Cage. The last time he'd been near the place, he'd carried his stepfather out the back door and away from the flailing fists of two men the old guy had offended.

That had been about six years ago, shortly after he and Maralynn had taken on the Kolstad Church. He hadn't had a difficult time explaining to her where he was going. She didn't know the names of bars, or anything about the seamy side of life.

But she had been repulsed and horrified at the beating he had taken, refusing to accept that he had come out of the melee in better shape than anyone else involved. Well, his stepfather had finally taken one drink too many and was now in Forest Cemetery, but it appeared that Hamish hadn't seen the last of the life he had been rescued from years ago.

If Brenda Jane wondered where he had grown his arm muscles, he could have told her street fighting and baseball, in that order. He apparently hadn't told her enough about his history. How much could he tell her, he wondered, before she turned away from him with distaste?

Waiting for Hamish was torturous. When everyone else had gone to bed, she sat in the living room with the TV sound turned off and listened to the pendulum of the small clock on the antique buffet. She slipped out of her chair and stretched out on the old plush couch with the lumpy padding.

Sitting in Hamish Chandler's living room was like stepping back half a century. She thought the furniture had probably been moved in with the first pastor way back when and had served each succeeding appointee to the present.

She studied each element of the room—the highly polished wood that nevertheless showed the wear of many little fingers, the heavy draperies, the old gilded mirror dull with age, probably worth a fortune today. Her gaze took in the leaded windows, beveled glass, wide-slatted maple floors with parquet corners, the heavy oak sliding doors always open between the living and dining rooms.

And then there were the personal touches like the vases, lamps and pictures most likely added by Hamish's wife.

Had Maralynn waited up for him on nights like this? What might it be like, B.J. wondered, to be the wife of a minister, to meet the expectations of the position, to wait for her husband while he dealt with the myriad responsibilities of his job? And the unexpected dangers?

She was determined not to think of the possibility of Hamish getting hurt at Grant's Cage. He had reassured her, and she already knew from what he had confided to her before that he just might be familiar enough with a place like that to handle himself there. Still, it was difficult to reconcile the Hamish she knew with the kind of person who could take care of himself in that part of town. She wondered just what his life had been like back then.

And, unbidden as if forbidden, the thoughts slipped in of being married to a man like Hamish Chandler, who unsparingly gave of himself to his friends and his congregation and who came home to hold a wife in his arms. She found her hands slick with sweat when she imagined being Hamish's wife in the night, deep in the night when it was just the two of them.

And then followed the dream-shattering reminders of meeting Edson Forda and Mrs. Deaton. Once again, B.J. felt inadequate, as if she wasn't only in the way of Hamish's finding a suitable wife, but that her sleeping in his home had compromised his reputation.

Hamish was going to find another woman to marry, to

bring to this house to mother his precious daughters and to share his bed. And his big, hard, sexy body and his big, gentle hands. She wouldn't care about the old furniture and the worn black places on the linoleum and the chipped wall-hung sink. Not when she could climb the stairs with him every night and know he was exclusively hers until morning.

Why did these images bring such aching?

It was after midnight when she heard Hamish come quietly through the back door. He walked into the living room in stocking feet and gazed down at her. She shifted her legs to make room for him. He hesitated for a moment, then sank wearily onto the other end of the couch and let his head fall back.

"I'm glad you're all right," she said.

"There wasn't anything for you to worry about," he replied.

"How can you say that? How can you think I wouldn't worry?" she demanded.

He inhaled wearily. "Brenda, I grew up in that part of town. I started dragging my stepfather home from places like Grant's Cage before I was twelve years old," he explained, his voice cracking with fatigue.

She stared at him in stunned silence, recognizing that he was revealing a part of his personal history he had never talked about before.

"I learned early how to take care of myself. I got my first job cleaning floors in one of those places when I was thirteen. The owner paid me cash under the table because it was illegal to hire me." He paused as if waiting for her to say something, and when she didn't, he continued his story. "I learned to be quick and alert, to watch over my shoulder at all times. And I learned other things, some of which you already know."

She saw his Adam's apple jerk as he swallowed and she reached out to clasp his hand. She could see he was telling her things he really didn't want her to know about him. But she wanted to hear it all. She wanted to know everything.

He lifted his head and turned to look at her. "I learned about drugs and making dirty money, lots of it. I learned about loyalty and betrayal and false love. And I learned what it was to have a bankrupt spirit, although I didn't know that's what it was at the time."

She struggled to reconcile the Hamish she knew with the desperate youth he was talking about. "Hamish, I'm sorry," she said, at a loss for words.

He hesitated, apparently surprised at her soft words, then he continued, "For seven years I lived like that, never getting caught at things that could have sent me to jail. I didn't know any other life. I thought there was no way out. And nobody seemed to care. Until one day when I met an undercover cop. I didn't know that's what he was until later, but I liked him and he liked me, and it was one of the first real friendships I made. He introduced me to baseball. Even in the sleazepit of the city, they had baseball leagues. When his assignment was over, he disappeared, of course, and no one thought much about it. But he came back into my life. He invited me to his home in the suburbs, and I sat down with his wife and children for dinner. Then I went back for a Sunday barbecue and a Fourth of July weekend. I began to experience things I'd never known before."

He turned his hand over and clasped hers, palm to palm. "He trusted me. I could have told a few people who he was, and he'd have been dead in a matter of hours. But I didn't. I couldn't. He trusted me." He paused to inhale slowly. "He saw something in me I didn't know was there. But I discovered later it had been there all along."

"So you turned yourself around," she observed, fascinated with the paradox that was Hamish Chandler.

"It wasn't so much a matter of turning myself around as seeing myself in a different way, getting to know myself, recognizing that what I secretly wanted out of life wasn't anywhere *in* my life until then. I met some of his friends. I got a job at one of those social service agencies where they hire young men to talk to street kids interested in having a better life. And I played baseball. I played on four different teams. I loved the game. I moved out of the old neighborhood, cut myself off from all that had once been familiar. And, I thought, hopeless.

"A scout for the Twins gave me a break, and I went to train with a farm team, then played in the minor leagues for a while. I started to really turn my life around. Then I met a minister who led me into a whole new world, one where I discovered who I was and who I wanted to be. Eventually I spent four years at a theological seminary in Kansas."

"I'm shocked," she said, shaking her head. "I thought you were just about the most naive man I'd ever met."

He grinned wearily. "I expected you to turn away in disgust, or maybe give me a lecture on what a hypocrite I am."

"Of all the labels I might hang on you, hypocrite is definitely not one of them," she told him, studying the strands of hair falling over his forehead and over his ears.

He rested his head back on the couch, and she watched him struggle through his memories.

"And your mother?" she asked.

"She died when I was young. I never knew who my father was."

She reflected briefly on how different the world might have been for many people if Hamish's violent career had not been interrupted by an undercover lawman.

She turned to him and spoke what was in her heart, without reservations or artifice. "I hope she can see how magnificently you turned out."

He rolled his head to face her, arching his eyebrows in amused disbelief. "At the very least, I expected a creative insult," he said.

She looked away, shrugging her shoulders. It was not a time for insults. He had revealed a past that astonished her, but she was not repulsed. His revelations only added another dimension to an already fascinating man.

"Tell me, what did you accomplish tonight?" she asked.

He paused. She felt his gaze on her. "I dragged one of my friends out of trouble and took him home," he said. "Neil has been a stable family man as long as I've known him, but last month his ten-year-old son nearly died in a car accident while Neil was driving. Something terrible is happening inside him. Tonight he just...went out to get drunk. And I think he was looking for a fight. Guilt, I guess. And rage."

"Is he in your congregation?"

"His wife is. He never joined."

"Then how did you talk him into going home?"

"I didn't. I offered to fight him on his own turf," he said. "He fell asleep in the car on the way home."

"Why, Hamish? Why would you do that?"

He shrugged. "I couldn't think of anything else right then."

"I mean, why go get him in the first place?"

He gave a short, humorless laugh. "There are a lot of people looking for answers, Brenda. I don't have the answers for them, but I want them to know it's important not to give up looking. It's what I learned. We all have choices, more than we realize."

Now that he was safely home and the tension was eased,

she moved into her chair to make her own way to bed. Once again, there was a tilt in her world, as her perception of Hamish Chandler revised itself yet again.

Hamish had never had a new car, B.J. learned. She'd already noticed that cars were not important to him, and these days he had better things to do than agree to take her car shopping. She never should have asked.

"Tammy loves shopping," he said. "I think she would love to take you to find a new car." She might have ignored his suggestion, but Tammy was standing beside him smiling, and there was little room for diplomatic maneuvering. She detected the slight tremble in Tammy's lower lip and a vague faltering of her sweet smile, but B.J. knew if Hamish wanted her to take his houseguest shopping, she would see it as her duty to do so.

She suspected that Tammy was as uncomfortable on a car lot as Hamish likely would have been, so she simply had Tammy drive slowly by a few dealers and made her choice from a distance. It was red and it was a two-seater, and by Hamish's standards, it was probably outrageously expensive. She would make the arrangements by telephone.

"Okay," she told Tammy. "It's done. What would you like to do now? Hamish said you like shopping."

"What? But you haven't bought a car yet."

"It's all done but the closing. I can take care of that later."

"I—I don't understand."

"Shopping. Where would you like to shop?"

Tammy stared at her in confusion for a long time and then smiled. "Christmas shopping," she blurted. "Wouldn't it be wonderful to go Christmas shopping together?"

B.J. was dumbfounded. It was only mid-October, and

Tammy had been talking about Christmas for weeks already. Hamish's congregation seemed to be obsessed with Christmas. They had been making quilts and crafts for months now.

But Christmas was something other people celebrated. Not her.

"All right," she conceded, blaming Hamish for suggesting their shopping trip in the first place.

Tammy pressed surefootedly on the gas pedal, B.J. noticed, then turned the wheel while she signaled, a confident, energetic action far removed from the slow, hesitant manner in which she had been driving up until now. She sped to the nearest discount department store and helped B.J. into her wheelchair.

It was a new experience for B.J.

"Oh, look, see? This is what little girls are wearing now," Tammy gushed, going through the children's clothing department as if each counter and rack held hidden treasures. "I hope I have a little girl. It will be such fun to make her pretty. Of course, I'll have to sew. We will never be able to afford these prices."

The prices seemed inordinately low to B.J.

"Ministers' children have to be nicely dressed," Tammy said, "but everyone knows exactly what your income is, and if you buy expensive clothes, well, they'll get a bad impression."

B.J. watched and listened in awe.

"I hope I can find something nice for Annie and Emma," Tammy said, digging carefully through a jumble of sweaters and other knit tops on a sale table. "Five dollars is my limit for children's gifts this year."

B.J. stared in disbelief.

"Of course, I'm making a lot of things."

"Making them?"

"Oh, yes. You know, like sewing little vests, and knitting some things like baby clothes and pot holders and those thick socks for some of the teens on our list. Home-knit things are so durable. Why, Annie is wearing some things Maralynn made for Emma years ago, and they don't even look worn.''

At the third discount store, B.J. rolled her chair away from Tammy for a while, impatient, disbelieving and disturbed by this view of what was expected of a pastor's wife. She felt like a stranger in a foreign country. Is that what they did? Knit and sew and cut corners, always calculating how to stretch every dollar? She knew some women knitted. Was it mandatory? She couldn't imagine knitting.

Maralynn had been the ''perfect'' pastor's wife and she had knitted clothes for her children. B.J. wheeled slowly down endless aisles with an urge to scream. She was outside the loop, an interloper in the life of a pastor. A misfit.

Then a sign caught her eye, and she stopped to look at the myriad scrunchies that girls wore to decorate their hair or simply keep it off their faces. She thought of Annie with her blond strands hanging in her eyes and hiding her face when she bent her head to read a picture book. She thought of Emma with her abundant curls, sometimes frizzy, overpowering her narrow features.

B.J. handled some of them, turned them over and inside out, then looked at them piece by piece. She was struck with an idea. She could see pastel shades of soft elastic velour in Annie's hair, and bright shiny reds and blues in Emma's. She could make them, she thought. It would be fun. She could buy the pieces—the ribbons, ties, elastic, bands—and glue, tie and pin them together. She could let the girls help, or at least watch.

She wasn't even thinking of Christmas. She was thinking of the girls. They'd enjoy the project and love the pretty decorations in their hair.

Maybe being part of a minister's family was an unfathomable thing that discouraged and mystified her, but she could be Hamish's daughters' friend and she could enjoy doing things with them. Even if Annie sat four feet away and Mrs. B had to arrange the finished scrunchie into her fine light hair.

Tammy was skeptical of B.J.'s purchases. "Whatever will you do with all those scraps?" she asked as they left the store. B.J. hid a secret smile. She wasn't bound by the conventions of a minister's wife. That was the silver lining, she thought sadly.

Hamish was late for dinner, and it was Meeting Night. He retreated to his study and shut the door to recover in privacy from a day that had been littered with aggravating incidents, disappointed people and frustrated objectives.

He was late in leaving for the church and was able to walk with his family, who usually left the house later than he did. Emma slipped onto Brenda's lap for a ride in the wheelchair. When they lagged behind, he turned to see that Brenda had allowed Emma to slow their speed in order to talk to a pouting Annie.

He should be running, he thought, but instead he stopped to watch and listen. Annie was feeling left out because Emma was riding on the chair. Yet when Brenda gently cajoled Annie to take a turn riding, the little girl pulled away sharply with a loud whine. It was a childish gesture that spurred his irritation with his youngest daughter.

Brenda, however, smiled in understanding and reached a hand out to touch Annie's arm. Annie slapped it away with a yelp. Hamish felt an urge to intervene, but he stayed still and observed. "All right," Brenda said, her voice more gentle and patient than Annie deserved. "If you change your mind, you tell me, okay? I would love to give you a ride. And Emma is willing to take turns with you."

"You're being icky, Annie," Emma chided. "Let's go, Brenda. Let's leave her in the dust."

"I care about you, Annie. I'd like to see you happy," Brenda said softly. "How about if we just ride slowly alongside you in case you change your mind?"

"Go 'way," Annie said, pouting, and Hamish hid a grin, remembering being faced with a similar reaction from the beautiful young woman in the wheelchair.

"I don't think so," Brenda said in a good-natured sing-song tone.

"C'mon, Brenda, let's just leave her," Emma was urging. "She's awful when she pouts."

He looked up to see Mrs. Billings waddling in a rush from the back door. "What's this?" she scolded, puffing as she approached them at the end of the driveway. "Shame on you, Annie. Keeping your father from his work when he's already late."

Annie's bright blue eyes widened in alarm and she turned to Hamish as if to ask, "What have I done?" He gave her a stern expression, and her chin quivered as she hurriedly searched the faces of the other three.

He was very late. He should be doing double time to the church, but he was enthralled with the little drama playing out before him. He watched as his younger child fought a familiar conflict with defiance, guilt and fear.

She jutted her chin in defiance, eyed him askance with guilt and conquered her fear. "Ride," she demanded. He noticed her little hands clenched into tight fists at her sides.

Brenda's smile lit the darkness beyond the yard light as she nudged a now-disgruntled Emma off her lap. Although Annie resisted Brenda's efforts to help her crawl up over her feet and onto her lap, Brenda waited happily, quickly reaching out to squeeze Emma's hand to share her victory.

"Do you want to drive?" she asked Annie, who jerked her head in the negative. She was perched on Brenda's knees as far away from her torso as she could get without falling off, and she tried to cross her arms, unwilling to give up being miffed.

Hamish might have rejoiced if he had dared, but he didn't want to spoil the moment. And, God knew, he was going to be starting the service unaccountably late, so he nodded briskly, suppressed a grin and broke away in a run.

He had been noticing in recent weeks how Brenda had been making efforts to reach Annie. It had occurred to him more than once that he should warn her that Annie was not like other children, that she was fearful, that her limited speech was not easily understood and that she was probably not as outgoing as many children her age.

Annie's riding on Brenda's lap was a major break-through, he thought, due totally to Brenda's loving persistence. He felt a surge of joy when he thought of the two of them together, both strong, independent and precious, but flawed and afraid, bringing out the best in each other.

After the prayer service, when people had scattered and the rooms were full of activity, he wandered the halls until he found her. He was astonished to see Brenda in the craft room bent over a table in conversation with two other women, one sitting across from her, reaching to manipulate some colorful material that seemed to be their focus, and the other standing beside Brenda's chair, leaning over to examine the same materials. Brenda's right arm was on the table, her fingers awkwardly curling around what appeared to be ribbons.

He stepped into the room, but none of the three women noticed, they were so intent. He closed in on them, approaching from behind Brenda's wheelchair. They still didn't seem to be aware he was there, but continued talking about hair and little girls.

He ambled casually out of the room with nods of greeting to several of the people mingling about and headed down the hall, away from the activity, to cut through the furnace room. It was a quick route to his office.

He needed some time alone. Brenda Jane Dolliver was driving him a little crazy, he thought, slipping into the corners of his life that he was only now realizing had been dark and silent for a long time.

He forgot his enchantment with Brenda Jane when he pulled into the driveway Thursday afternoon behind a new red sports car. He hadn't asked how her car shopping had gone yesterday because frankly he had forgotten about it.

Now he could only think, My God, Brenda, what have you done? He hurried to the house. As soon as he opened the back-porch door, his daughters slammed into him, and he hugged them and lifted them into his arms.

"We got something new to ride in!" Emma squealed. "It's bright bright bright red!"

"Red," Annie echoed.

"I saw it," he told them wryly, then exchanged a "What next?" glance with Mrs. B in the kitchen. Couldn't Brenda have waited until she was out of his house to get the car? It hadn't occurred to him that she would park a flashy sports car in his driveway, displayed for all his congregation to see. He intended to let her know what this would cost him.

When he found her at the dining-room table, he recognized the colorful clutter before her. He had seen part of it on the craft-room table last night. The sight caused him to come to an abrupt stop. His daughters slid into chairs on either side of Brenda and joyously immersed their eager hands into the snarls of colorful paraphernalia.

He was speechless.

Brenda was making intricate yet girlish ornaments for

their hair. Three of them already sat off to the side, looking tasteful and attractive.

"Daddy's home now. Can we show him?" Emma prodded anxiously.

"Me try this one," Annie said, pointing to the arrangement Brenda was working on.

Brenda looked up at him, her brilliant smile radiating electric darts that skewered his heart. He thought for an instant it had actually stopped beating.

"Hi, Hamish," she greeted.

He sank onto the chair at the end of the table. He tried to say hi, but no sound came out.

He watched Brenda put the finishing touches to the ornament, working slowly, using her right hand to steady and hold it. She offered it to Annie, who took it carefully in her two hands, then walked slowly, as if it were as fragile as an egg, to have Mrs. B put it into her hair.

Brenda pulled Emma's hair into a ponytail on the crown of her head and slipped on a bright teal-and-red bowlike decoration to hold it there. His older daughter suddenly seemed prettier without the mass of curls crowding her features. She took on a maturity that was a little frightening to him as a father.

Annie's hair was pulled to the side, the soft colors of the ribbons making her look like an angel.

They paraded and preened in front of him and baited him for praise, which he gave eagerly and affectionately. When he had them both in his arms, he looked over their heads at Brenda, who was smiling as she studied her handiwork. He remembered how Maralynn used to make things for the girls, practical things like sweaters and mittens, done with an absence of fanfare.

He loved the way the girls were giggling. The way Mrs. B was cooing over them, the way Brenda was smiling. He felt so happy and grateful he wanted to lean over and kiss Brenda on the lips and tell her she was terrific.

He knew her mouth would be warm and soft, and he knew he wanted more than kisses. He also knew that something strange and new, and erotically sensual, was happening to him.

Some other time he would talk to her about the car.

Chapter Eight

Now that her right arm was gaining strength, B.J. was able to use the crutches. It was frightening at first. She felt high and unstable, as if she were standing on precarious stilts, but she forced herself to walk, and the fear subsided as she gained confidence. Although she wasn't capable of taking a step without the crutches, she could move nearly anywhere with them.

And now that she had the car and could drive it, she was able to start visiting the rehab center by herself without waiting for the van.

That there was no progress in her condition did not discourage her. Nor did the nagging pain in her side, the pain that recently had begun shooting down her leg.

Since her arrival at the Chandler household, she had not missed a Wednesday Meeting Night, and now that the weather was too cold for softball, she watched her new friends play volleyball in the all-purpose room.

One night, Les Johnson gestured to her to join in, and she responded. She stood behind the white line and served a powerful left-handed shot only slightly out of control into the opposition court. He let her serve in his place until someone on his team knocked it out of bounds. All the players cheered when he handed her the crutches and she made her way back to the sidelines.

It felt like her greatest athletic achievement, although it reminded her that in reality she was never going to be the athlete she had been before the accident. The friendships were valuable, however, as was the support of people she hadn't even wanted to meet two months earlier. Their cheers touched something in her.

What a paradox, she thought. Friendship had never been of much value to her.

Neither had family—except for her father, who had not really known her.

When the volleyball game was over, she walked to the children's rooms and looked in on the small groups of youngsters, roughly divided by age. Legions of moms stood around talking with each other, intermittently tending to the children, while some were engrossed in working with the little ones on cutouts or clay.

She waved to Emma, who was cutting something into strips. And then she wandered to Annie's room, where she found the child rubbing her eyes. She warily approached her and was warmed when Annie raised her arms up to her. She felt a kind of thrill from the unfamiliar gesture of trust.

She quickly sat on a small chair and laid her crutches on the floor. Annie crawled up on her lap, laying her cheek against B.J.'s breast. Within a few short minutes, her eyes closed, and B.J. felt her body relax until she was limp. She felt a catch in her chest when she looked down at the child sleeping against her breast.

"I was about to look for Pastor," one of the women

said, squatting beside her. "I hope Annie isn't coming down with something."

"I'll just hold her for a while. I'm...Brenda Dolliver," she said.

"I know. I'm Gloria Newsom. Nice to see you've graduated to crutches."

"Thanks. But if I had my chair, I could carry her home," B.J. said.

"I'll find Pastor," Gloria said.

It was the last thing B.J. wanted, to give up her sweet, soft burden. "No," she replied. "Really, it isn't necessary. We'll be going home soon anyway."

B.J. looked around the room and watched the children drawing, sprinkling sparkling specks on glue, playing games. Several children in one corner were playing musical chairs very noisily. When there was an outburst, she looked down at the sleeping child in her arms and rubbed her back the way Hamish did.

She wondered what it would be like to hold her own child. She wondered what it would be like to hold a child that was hers and Hamish's. The thought of Hamish loving her until he gave her a baby made something tighten in her belly.

That thought brought back the ache that had haunted her more frequently these days, an ache unbearably sweet and pointedly painful. And every day, it ground into her more deeply, stirring things deep inside.

Her right side was beginning to throb and a pain shot down her leg, but she wouldn't give up her beloved burden. She used her hand to change the position of her leg, although it didn't seem to help. Ignore it, she told herself, looking at Annie's upturned nose and her long blond hair.

She touched Annie's forehead. It was warm, but not hot. Surely the child was just sleepy and not ill.

Then Hamish came striding powerfully through the

door. He dropped with lithe grace to his haunches, concern and warmth radiating from his face. His hand went instinctively to Annie's forehead.

"She's not sick, just tired," B.J. whispered.

"She looks so comfortable I hate to disturb her, but I'd better get her off your lap," he said softly, then reached to pick her up, brushing his hand along her breasts. The touch startled him as much as it did her. He froze for just a second, met her gaze and lifted Annie against his chest, her cheek resting on his shoulder.

He extended a hand to help B.J. to her feet. When she moved, a sharp pain shot through her side and down her leg again, and she winced. "I think I'll sit here for a few minutes," she said, forcing a weak smile.

"You're in pain," he said, frowning.

"I just need to rest for a few minutes. I'll be fine," she told him, wondering why it should still hurt and if it would indeed diminish if she stretched it out, now that Annie's weight was gone.

"Are you sure about that?"

"Oh, yes, it happens sometimes. See to Annie. I'll be along."

"Send for me if you need help," he said, and carried Annie out.

A woman who had been helping the boy across the table looked up and asked, "Are you all right?"

"It's nothing, just a cramp."

Maybe it was a cramp, she thought, straightening with difficulty. Well, she had withstood greater pain than this and she could certainly ignore it for now. But every step she took caused a sharp twinge, even when she bent her right leg so that it didn't touch the ground.

She found Mrs. Billings and Emma just as someone came to tell them that Hamish had walked home with a sleeping Annie in his arms.

They started the trek to the house then, and less than a third of the way there, she told Mrs. Billings to go ahead, that she was tired and wanted to take it easy. It was obvious Mrs. Billings was anxious to get to Annie. She and Emma scurried ahead, disappearing down the drive, holding hands.

I can take this pain, she told herself. But it was difficult making her way. She stopped after every few steps. As cars started leaving the church, she found an excuse to stop frequently to step out of the road. When she finally reached the highway, she geared up to cross it in one stretch. Then she stopped on the other side and waved to people coming from the church road.

Getting to the house was agony, but she made it. In the driveway, she met Hamish on his way back to the church. His face took on a bluish cast under the yard light. "Are you all right?" he asked.

"I'm fine," she replied.

"Mrs. Billings is putting Annie to bed. I'm glad you were there to hold her when she needed someone." He paused. "I'm glad it was you she went to," he added softly.

Not a single acid barb came to mind to cover up how profoundly his words affected her. In fact, she almost said "Amen" to his acknowledging that she had finally crossed the barrier Annie had erected between them. She moved her gaze to the house, where she could see Mrs. Billings moving through the living room in the golden glow of the lights.

"I heard that you made four points in a volleyball game tonight," he said, grinning. "Even only using your left arm."

"Les Johnson let me take his serve."

"He said he wants to be on your team when you get rid of the crutches."

She replied absently, "I should have accepted your challenge in darts."

He laughed and escorted her into the house. She tried to keep up, but had to stop before they reached the ramp. "You're not fine," he said.

"I'm just tired," she replied. He nodded grimly and left to see that the church was closed up.

He carried her up the stairs later that night and held her longer than was necessary before he set her on the edge of the bed. She wanted him to lie down with her. But she knew he wouldn't.

After everyone was in bed, she got up and dug into her bag for the pain pills she had never expected to use again. They helped her sleep.

The next morning at the rehab center, the therapist called Dr. Wahler because B.J. found it too painful to undergo her usual routine. The doctor set up an appointment for her the next day for an examination.

She returned home feeling discouraged, depressed, fearful and sorry for herself. Her side now throbbed continuously, and when she walked, the sharp pain was stronger than ever.

Annie was sitting at the table sucking on a soda cracker when she entered the kitchen. "I frew up," she said proudly.

B.J. gave her a hug and a smile, both of which Annie returned for the first time. "I'm very tired," she told Mrs. Billings. "I think I'll take a nap." She took another pain pill and went to bed, wishing she could sleep until her appointment the next day. Mrs. Billings came in at dinnertime to ask how she was feeling. "I think I have an upset stomach," she lied. "I just want to sleep."

The next morning, B.J. drove to her appointment and requested a wheelchair the minute she was inside the main entrance of the hospital. Afterward, she drove to a parking lot along the Mississippi River and sat for a long time, watching the tugs and pleasure craft on the fast-flowing murky water below. It was quiet, and she needed to think. And cry.

She had been leaning on Hamish, taking advantage of his generous spirit, taking everything he gave—his time, his attention, his concern. And now, after all this time, she was taking a large step backward, and she would be leaning on him more heavily than ever to start another recovery. It wasn't just the medical setback that was bringing her to her knees. It was the ache inside her, the consequences of having one Hamish Chandler in her life. It was the painful awareness that she could be with him only as long as she was dependent upon him. As long as she was taking advantage of his kindness, she could live in his house, look at him across the table, watch him on Wednesday nights, feel his occasional touch, listen to him laugh. And while she held on to him, he waited for her to get well so that he could get on with his life and find someone he might love enough to marry.

She didn't want to tell him about the upcoming operation.

She didn't want to tell him she would be back in the hospital again, starting over.

She didn't want to think about it. But she could think of nothing else.

Hamish hadn't seen Brenda since Wednesday night, and now it was Friday afternoon. Even Mrs. Billings was concerned. "She's been in her room or gone somewhere," she told him. "And when she's here, she isn't herself."

"Call me when she comes home. You have no idea where she is?"

"She said she had an appointment, but that was at ten this morning."

"It will be all right," he replied, strangely disturbed. It was like a warning, and it haunted him. "Call me if you hear from her."

It had been impossible to concentrate after that, and so he did what he always did when he felt unsettled. He went to church.

As he approached the altar he stopped, for there she knelt on the steps, her head bowed, shoulders hunched, a position very familiar to him. Her crutches were lying at odd angles on the floor behind her, as if she had let them fall.

He inhaled sharply at the catch in his chest and swallowed hard before he started toward her, stepping quietly. He was sure she must hear him, for the silence was overwhelming. Every creak and groan of the structure was audible.

When he stood directly behind her, she spoke, her voice full of anguish in the powerful silence. "Hamish?"

"I'm here," he replied softly.

"I thought it might help me. I know it helps you. But I can't do it," she cried.

"Can't do what, Brenda?"

She twisted around and sat on the step she had been kneeling on. "I don't know how to pray," she whispered tragically.

In astonishment, he sat on the step beside her. "Just speak as you would to one with whom you have a relationship."

"I don't have a relationship with God, Hamish," she said. "I never have. I don't know where to find Him."

"Well, just make yourself available, Brenda, and let Him find you," he said, reaching over to pull her against him. Her head fell against his shoulder where it fitted perfectly. "You've been dreading the moment when I bring out the Good Book and start telling you about sin and grace and how to worship and list all the reasons you should be joining this church and attending Sunday services," he said. "Haven't you?"

"I was ready with all my arguments. But you defused them by not preaching to me, and now here I am, wondering if there's something here for me."

"What's brought this on, Brenda? What happened?"

She curled against him and held her tongue, but he wasn't going to press her. He knew what it was like to begin the search and he wasn't about to be heavy-handed with her fragile efforts. Besides, there was more going on between them than friendship, and he recognized his responsibility to be true to himself.

When he felt she was slipping away from him, when he feared she was going to withdraw, he pulled away and said that Mrs. Billings was worried about her and would like her to come home.

"I'm leaving next week," she said, looking down at something on the steps. "I'll be gone for about a week. I'm going to visit my father."

"So you've finally called him."

"I've written to him. I just didn't tell him about the accident."

"Until now?"

She ignored his question, but he refrained from challenging. "He's in California. He's opening another store in Long Beach."

"Will you be coming back?" he asked very carefully, wondering with a sinking heart what he would do if she didn't come back.

"I'm planning to. If I'm still welcome."

"You'll always be welcome. You're like part of the family now. When you leave, we'll all feel the loss," he told her, hoping she believed it.

"Until you marry again," she murmured.

"Even then," he said, his throat tightening around the words. "But that's a long way off."

"Maybe not. You never know...when..." She left the thought hanging.

"Very true. One never knows," he agreed. But he knew one thing. He had lost his enthusiasm for looking elsewhere for a wife. Green eyes and rich brown hair and a little healing scar on her cheek now filled his vision.

He hadn't seen her for forty-eight hours and he had missed her. He'd been distracted by not seeing her and had felt uncomfortable not knowing where she was all day. Last night, it had seemed as though half his family was missing when she wasn't at the dinner table.

The silence between them was heavy and sad, and he longed to tell her that he wanted her to come back as soon as she could. He wondered why she was unhappy and why she wanted to leave. But she wasn't going to answer those questions—at least, not now.

"When will you be leaving?" he asked instead.

"Next Wednesday, very early, before anyone is up."

"Then we have you for four whole days yet," he said.

The following afternoon when B.J. returned from shopping, Hamish was already home. "Picnic time," he said as she flopped a newly purchased scrapbook on the kitchen table. "What's this?"

"It's for me," she said. "I've decided to put some of my work into it." A slow smile spread over his face, and she knew he was thinking about the newspaper clippings he had slipped into the bottom of the suitcase the day he'd gone to her apartment for clothes. He smiled at her and she smiled back. "Thanks for bringing them," she said softly, acknowledging for the first time that he had done so.

"You're so very welcome, dear lady," he said, grinning.

"And what's this about a picnic? It's practically winter. Nobody has picnics this time of year."

"You might not have noticed, but fall is making a remarkable last-ditch effort to impress us today. It's probably the last warm day until next May. We're going to have a picnic. By the St. Croix River." He looked boyish. She wanted to throw her arms around him.

Instead she joined in with preparations for the picnic, helping and watching Mrs. B boil potatoes and eggs, raiding leftovers, wrapping up hot dogs, retrieving frozen buns from the freezer. B.J. and Annie made a cake, but it didn't rise, so they cut it up into bars and frosted it anyway.

Mrs. Billings did a last-minute inventory, grabbed napkins and put a couple of wet washcloths in plastic sacks. Then they headed for the St. Croix River.

Hamish knew just the spot where there had at one time been a landing. The banks were sandy and sloped gently to the water. The autumn leaves had fallen from the trees, and the unseasonably warm wind blew the dry, colored remnants around their feet.

The mood was festive. And Hamish was a happy man, surrounded by the people he loved most. While they sat around the food on the blankets, he looked up at the clear, pale blue sky and felt profound gratitude for the day and for the moment.

When Brenda's gaze locked with his, he felt his joy expressing itself from the inside out, for there was something deep and serious and warm in her eyes today, and it banished his presentiment of darker times ahead.

After they'd eaten, he sprawled on one edge of the blanket and looked across at Brenda. She lay with her head propped on an elbow. Emma was lazily draped over her, his daughter's chin resting on Brenda's neck, their hair

tangling together in the warm breeze. They were speaking
softly about something, and Hamish was mesmerized. Annie sprawled on her back in the curl of Brenda's body with
her knees bent over Brenda's thighs. Unafraid. Comfortable.

She might have been their loving mother, the picture
they made, easy and relaxed, folded around one another,
and Hamish found his breath stuck somewhere in his chest.
He didn't need to look far for a mother for his daughters.
But if he was looking at her in terms of a wife, he knew
it was unlikely that Brenda would ever be interested.

It was clear his daughters loved her—even Annie, who
had put up a good fight. He didn't know exactly when it
had happened, although he should have guessed it would,
given the change in Brenda Jane. There was a gentleness
in her now that he hadn't seen before, and sometime during
the past two months, she had wormed her way into the
hearts of both of his children.

It couldn't last, of course. The sports car alone was a
symbol, a reminder of the kind of life Brenda would be
returning to. There would be no place in that life for a
humble husband with a run-down farmhouse and a family
accustomed to getting along with minimal comforts.

He felt an impulse to gather the three of them in his
arms and hold them there.

Mrs. Billings's sigh distracted him. "Everything's just
about perfect, isn't it?" she said.

He felt a kind of conditional joy bubble out of him.
"That it is," he replied softly, but when he looked at
Brenda he saw shadows in her face.

It wasn't until Hamish had left the house Sunday morning that B.J. announced to Mrs. Billings and the girls that
she was going to accompany them to church. She took a
pain pill before leaving the house, rode her chair to the

church and walked inside on her crutches so that she could sit in a pew like everyone else.

It wasn't that she just wanted to attend the service, she reminded herself. It was rather that she wanted to see Hamish in his collar and vestment conducting the formal service, not just the short ten-to-fifteen minute prayer meeting she witnessed on Wednesday nights. She wanted to see him at his job.

Maybe he saw himself as some kind of servant to the people who owned his church, but she knew he was a leader, a unique, compassionate, competent leader devoted to his responsibilities and to his family.

In the time she had been in his home, she had seen the way people treated him. They cared for him, respected him, held him in a kind of awe that he never seemed to notice. They called him when they were in trouble and jumped readily to his side when he asked for assistance. It was ironic, she thought, that of all the men she had ever considered heroes, she was so affected by a man like Hamish Chandler who laughed at her insults and thought he was rich.

If he was surprised to see her there, he didn't express it, but smiled at her in welcome when he first greeted the congregation.

She felt tears stinging her eyes and fought them back during the singing. The music roared through the church, the organ and the voices reflecting zeal and harmony.

After the service, the all-purpose room was transformed into a cafeteria where coffee, juice and baked goods were served. Children ran among the tables and people lingered over half-empty cups. Teenagers gathered, boys and girls being shy and bold, laughing and whispering. And the elderly mixed with the rest, oohing at how tall little Edward had grown, how tragic it was that Mrs. McKay's son had moved his family away. They all knew Emma and Emma knew many of them. She wound her way among them with Annie trailing, half-hiding, gifting them with her shy smiles.

Les Johnson came by and put a heavy hand on B.J.'s shoulder, then teased her about her powerful volleyball serve. Two of the women from Annie's room on Wednesday night stopped to inquire how Annie was.

They like me, she thought, and I haven't done a thing to impress them. She hadn't intended to belong here. She hadn't intended anything but to use Hamish's hospitality to recuperate and then be on her way.

But she did belong.

For the first time in her life, she belonged without white-knuckled effort.

She tried to sort it out, all the things that were overwhelming her—her growing dependence on Hamish, learning a new way of life, leaving behind all that had been familiar, relying on others because she was crippled, finally finding a home after all these years, facing the surgeon again next Wednesday morning. God, it was bittersweet.

The trembling started somewhere beyond her consciousness and spread through her chest and her limbs, a trembling that came from the core of her being and wouldn't stop.

She excused herself from the table and went home, distraught, shivering and frightened.

Where's my fight? she wondered. Where's my toughness? What's happening to me? It was a cocoon she was spinning around herself, she decided, to keep herself safe from the vague, intimidating future where she couldn't see what hid in the shadows.

Chapter Nine

This is where I came in, Hamish thought, looking down upon her sleeping form. It was a different room in the hospital, and there was no trapeze bar, but the plastic bags hooked to her were dripping and she was lying very still. Her face was lovely, her skin clear of bruises and abrasions. Only the small jagged scar interrupted the classic lines of her cheek.

He held her fingers against his lips and drank in her scent, hoping for an easing to whatever tormented her soul.

No, this was a far place from where he had first entered her life as a dispassionate observer, a stranger come to tangle with a feisty lioness he had come to call dear lady.

While he sat at her bedside, he remembered his first few visits, the passion that sprang up like magical beanstalks to tie him in knots, her call in the middle of the night to rescue her, his visit to her chic condo, her first days in his home, the night she massaged his neck and he discovered he had never before wanted any woman with quite the intensity he wanted her, the Wednesday nights she followed him and watched, the tumble from the shed loft, the night she held the sleeping Annie to her breast, the desperation in her cry that she didn't know how to pray, and last weekend.

Ah, yes, last weekend. Now that had been something to fill his heart, watching her creatively minimize her failure to bake a cake, sprawling on a blanket with her and his children, experiencing the fullness of having her in his life.

On Tuesday night, he had discovered her secret. He had suspected something wasn't right for several days before the mysterious telephone call. And when the voice on the telephone sounded more official than friendly, and when Brenda wanted to take the call in private, he *knew* she was hiding something important. He never did find out whom the call was from, but it incited him into action. She was going away, all right, but not to her father's, he'd discovered after a few strategic inquiries.

What he didn't understand was why she couldn't bring herself to tell him. He was disappointed that she hadn't trusted him.

When finally her eyelids fluttered open, she frowned at him in confusion. "Am I dying?" she whispered.

"I hope not," he said, smiling.

"Why...you here?" She spoke in the husky whisper he had come to know so well during his initial visits to her in the hospital. She spoke now with difficulty, obviously fighting the medication.

"Why not?" he asked. "Why are you surprised?"

"How...?"

"Let it be a lesson, Brenda Jane. You can't keep secrets from me," he warned, grinning at her bewilderment.

Her fingers curled weakly around his hand. She sighed and closed her eyes.

It was an hour later before she was alert enough to talk

to him, but he waited gladly, unable to leave her side, reluctant to be more than a foot or two away from her.

"Do what you did before," she murmured.

"What thing?" he asked, raising his eyebrows suggestively.

"Warm cloth. On my face."

He remembered that well, and how it had relaxed her. "If you promise not to fall asleep while I'm trying to talk to you," he said.

"No promises, Hamish."

"Well, I want to talk to you, Brenda Jane. I'm in the mood for negotiating." He lay the warm washcloth over her forehead.

"Negotiating?"

"You tell me why you didn't want me here, and I'll tell you how I found out about your little secret."

She handed him back the washcloth, placing it respectfully into his palm, and he recognized again how different she was from the cranky patient who had simply flung it over the side of the bed.

"I've been using you, Hamish, taking advantage of your goodness, taking you away from your work, causing you stress. I put you out of your own bed, for heaven's sake, and forced you to put your life on hold." She avoided his eyes while she spoke, but he watched her face, her lower lip quivering slightly.

"I haven't put my life on hold," he corrected.

"Parts of it you have," she insisted quietly. "You can't afford the time to look for a wife when I'm depending on you."

"Well, that's very true, but I don't mind," he replied, and wondered whether he ought to tell her how he felt, that he didn't want to look elsewhere. Would she feel trapped by his feelings for her? Would she feel she had to get away from him, from the confines of his house, if his intentions went beyond assisting her to recuperate? When she was well, he knew, she would hate the shabby simplicity of his life.

"You're too good to me, Hamish. No one has ever taken care of me like that before. No one has ever ca...been the friend you have."

"Thank you. I truly am your friend, and I still don't understand why you didn't tell me."

She looked down, blinking away the hint of tears. "All you've done for me so far has been for nothing, don't you see? I'm back where I started. I'm not getting better. I'm not keeping up my end of the bargain."

"What bargain are you speaking of? I don't remember any bargain that said you have to walk by a certain date or all arrangements are off. Did we make a bargain like that?" He didn't mean for his voice to sound harsh, but he was beginning to see that she felt unworthy, and he didn't like it.

Her eyes flashed open and her gaze hooked into his. She tapped fingers against her chest. "It was in here, that bargain. I'd never have imposed on you, Hamish, if I thought it was going to be long-term."

He leaned closer. "The only deal we made was that you would not offend my family or congregation. There was never a time limit. There were no expectations between us as far as your recovery was concerned. You have no right to impose your own private expectations on me, Brenda Jane Dolliver, and I won't accept them."

He watched the struggle taking place within her as she analyzed his words and sorted through her own thoughts and feelings. He was willing to gamble that she hadn't quite seen things as he presented them, but had been so wrapped up in her own pain and disappointment and sinking self-esteem that she had gotten everything screwed around so that it seemed to make sense.

Then again, he wanted to direct things to suit his own agenda, he reminded himself, and it wasn't fair of him to judge what she had decided for herself. He wanted her back in his home, eating at his table, sleeping in his bed—even though he wasn't in it—waiting up for him when he was late, asking about his day.

He longed for her. He'd seen her buttering the girls' toast, sharing hugs at bedtime. He wanted her to become dependent, so dependent that she would never want to leave. He wanted to wrap her in his love so that she would never want to escape, so that she would never know she was imprisoned, fastened to him for the rest of her life.

Fat chance, he reminded himself.

Her lips moved, but she failed to speak.

"Do you understand?" he asked, gentling his voice.

"No, I don't understand at all, but I'm willing to admit that you probably do, and that eventually I will," she said slowly, thoughtfully. Then with a puckish grin, she added, "I was coming back. I can prove it."

"Oh?"

"I bought you a present," she said, holding her smile. "It's in that skinny door with the holes. I was going to give it to you when I came back...from visiting my father in California."

He reached behind him and found a brown paper sack hiding a gift-wrapped box about ten inches long and two inches high. The paper was glossy brown, very masculine, and the bow was black, very elegant. With his elbows on his thighs, he held it loosely in his hands between his spread knees, weighing it, staring at it.

"Open it," she said, her smile reaching to her eyes.

He unwrapped it carefully because it was the classiest package he'd ever received, then he lifted the lid of the box to find two dozen soft white handkerchiefs with his monogram in the corner.

Looking into her eyes, he knew his mouth was hanging open. And for one of the few times in his life, he was speechless.

"I owe you," she said, laughing, then winced from the effort. "I use more of your handkerchiefs than you do. I should have put my own initials on them."

He raised himself enough to lean over and kiss her lingeringly on the lips. "Thank you," he whispered into her soft mouth. "I've never had such fine ones."

B.J. came home on crutches, free of most pain except for the soreness from the surgery, and she slipped back into the Chandler home. When she stepped from Hamish's car, his two little girls flew from the house and then stopped abruptly before they could slam into her. Obviously, they had been warned to go easy on the recovering patient. They wrapped little arms around her gently. Hamish stood close behind her, evidently expecting her to need his support. Instinctively, she covered her tender surgical site with her right hand. Little arms continued to hug her tightly.

"Brenda! Brenda!" they squealed.

"We missed you soooo much," Emma said.

Her back was pressed full length against Hamish, his fingers curled around her shoulders, the heat from him penetrating through her clothes, distracting her from the girls' embraces. "Careful, girls," he was saying over her shoulder. "Careful now."

He handed her the fallen crutches and took the girls' hands so that she could walk into the house on her own. Mrs. Billings met her at the door with another long hug. "It's so good to have you home," she said.

Home.

She *was* home.

She looked around the kitchen at all the chips and worn

spots and old things that she had silently derided on first arriving and wondered how they could have bothered her so much.

Hamish's fingers curled around her shoulders again as he stood behind her in the kitchen. "It seemed like a month," he said softly in her ear. "Welcome home."

His heat took the breath from her, so she only nodded in reply and attempted to compose herself.

How could it have seemed a month to him? He had visited her every afternoon and called her every morning over the past three days. Still, it was nice to know he missed her. He was a thoughtful, caring man, and she had better remember that he treated everyone with thoughtful caring. And however much the place felt like home, and however sincerely they greeted her, this was *not* her permanent home. Her stay was temporary.

Truth be known, she felt she could have gone to her place in downtown Minneapolis and lived alone with little hardship. Thank heavens the Chandlers didn't think she could get along without them, and so the condo hadn't been an option.

That night when she slipped between the sheets, she knew Hamish had slept in the bed while she was gone. The sheets were clean and everything was in order, but there was something...just something. A faint scent of him from the blankets maybe, or just the feeling that his large body had lain there last night and the nights before that.

In spite of her fatigue, she lay awake a long time with unwanted thoughts. Someday, Hamish would lie in this bed with a wife, another woman, and Brenda Jane Dolliver would be out of his life, only a memory.

She simply wasn't wife material. Even Mrs. Deaton had hinted at that. Just as well, she thought. Just as well. Even if she wanted to marry him, he wouldn't have her.

* * *

In the week that followed, she made remarkable progress. As the surgical soreness disappeared, she found her right side stronger and felt more agile than she had at any time since the accident. She returned to therapy and began, for the first time in months, to see some progress.

She was proving the doctors wrong. She had known all along she could do it. She was going to walk under her own power, and she was going to do it soon.

It was an exhilarating thought.

Reality, though, had its dark side. When she was obviously able to take care of herself, she would be obligated to leave.

Working on her scrapbook proved to be inspiring, and Mrs. Billings and the children enjoyed it for an hour or so each afternoon.

One night at dinner, Emma said, "Daddy, Brenda went over the ocean to take pictures of little children starving and people shooting guns."

"Yes, I know," he replied.

"She's a fographer."

"Photographer."

"Brenda, can you take pictures of us?"

B.J. looked around the table and thought of her cameras back in her condo. She hadn't touched them in months. "Why, yes, I suppose I could," she said to Emma, and thought of all the times she had pictured the girls in photographs, the times she had imagined capturing their moods and expressions. Mostly, she had thought about photographing Hamish, with his collar and without it, reading stories to his daughters, swinging a baseball bat. "I'll get my cameras," she murmured, already planning poses and lighting and expressions she wanted to capture. It would be something to take with her when she left, the Chandlers living their lives, photographs to remind her of the happiest time she had ever known.

A family album of sorts, which would include her.

The suggestion proved to be another turning point for her because once she had a camera in her hand, she couldn't stop using it. There were obstacles, of course, frustrating obstacles because she couldn't get into the positions she would have liked if she had been physically able. She resented her lack of agility and the way it limited her camera work.

One night, she spent a silent hour simply taking shots of Hamish reading stories to his daughters. Another time, she captured the severe tension in his face before he rushed out the door to once again rescue Neil Haraldson from his self-destructive guilt.

Several times, she wandered to the church to take pictures of committee meetings and Hamish working at his desk. After taking a picture of him praying alone at the altar, she was properly, if gently, chastised. He cupped her face in his hands and said softly, but with a tone that brooked no argument, "Some things are private, Brenda." He also wouldn't permit her to bring her camera into the church during services.

She finally found an opportunity to get photos of him in his collar, the kind of photos she wanted, when she crashed a wedding at the church one Saturday afternoon and was barely noticed among all the shutterbugs.

On Meeting Nights, she took pictures of quilters and crafters and volleyball players, of small children, large children, parents and senior citizens.

She took photographs of the church in the early morning after a snowfall when the trees and roofs were laden with white lace, and at night when it was glowing gold.

She took pictures of Hamish comforting Annie after one of the maturing but well-loved kittens was given away, another of him handing Emma her forgotten backpack when the school bus stopped at the end of the driveway one frosty morning.

Another morning while he was shaving in the upstairs bathroom and had left the door ajar, she took photos of him wearing only a towel wrapped around his hips. He objected, but she stopped clicking only because she was hypnotized by the sight of his virile, half-naked body, his broad, square shoulders, large, graceful muscles, lightly bearded chest and hard, flat stomach. She backed slowly out of the room, her tongue stuck to the roof of her mouth.

She took pictures of him when he was weary and when he was happy, when he was eating and when he was working. She didn't take pictures of him, however, when he was sleeping. With one exception. One night, she looked up from the TV to see him sound sleep, as were the girls, one on each knee. She took shots from at least half a dozen angles.

After Thanksgiving, she took her box of film to her editor, even though she was on medical leave, and he agreed to let her use the newspaper's darkroom. She offered to pay for its use, but when she showed him the contact sheets she'd printed, he was fascinated with the story of Kolstad Church's handsome widower pastor, who had been a minor league baseball player.

"Are all churches like this?" he asked her. "Seems as though the place is run by committees. It looks like a center to wrap your life around. Is this for real? Yuppies and farmers and single welfare mothers and families. Men's club, Bible study, volleyball, counseling sessions, weddings, funerals, baptisms, religious education, a task force for this and a task force for that. Are all churches like this?"

"I don't know," she replied. "I suppose so."

"Let me hang on to these for a while, okay?"

"No problem. I'll make another set of contact sheets,"

she told him. They were fairly easy and quick to make.
The newspaper used them to make photo selections for
publication. B.J. intended to make prints herself—some to
frame, some for a "family" album of memories.

Her boss talked about her coming back to work part-
time, but she didn't feel capable of moving around with
the agility she thought she would need to do a good job,
so she asked for more time.

"Let's talk about it in January," she suggested. "And
I won't be ready for news assignments for a long time."
Maybe she could handle some feature stuff, she thought,
as long as she could take her time to get the angles she
wanted.

The day was getting closer when she would have to
leave her newfound family, and it stung. The more mobile
she became, the more it hurt to think of the future. Her
position in the family, ironically, seemed to be solidifying.
When Hamish left in the mornings, he kissed all three of
them goodbye, and when he returned at night, he sometimes hugged them all, B.J. included.

He touched her more often, too, smoothing her hair or
brushing a tangled strand off her face, or simply running
his large, warm hands down her arms from her shoulders.
Every touch ignited a spark deep inside, and she longed
for more.

At the same time, she interpreted his gestures as accep-
tance of her place in his life as a dear friend, a houseguest.
She saw it as a signal from him that he no longer desired
her, that it was safe to treat her as he treated his children
and his close friends, with wholesome affection.

He might as well have shouted that he was no longer
attracted to her.

No longer attracted in *that* way, at least.

Her life, although it seemed finally to be grounded in
sanity, was one of contradictions. And it was moving in-

exorably to a moment she dreaded more than she had ever
dreaded anything in her life—leaving Hamish forever.

B.J. was standing in the kitchen when it happened. She
actually slid her right foot forward and moved her left foot
up to it. Without crutches. Without leaning on anything.

She had taken a step on her own!

Admittedly, it wasn't a real, lifting, heel-first step, but
it was the beginning of one. It was the beginning of walking on her own.

B.J. wanted to scream her success. Mrs. Billings's back
was turned, and Emma was setting the table. Hamish was
washing up in the downstairs bathroom and Annie was
watching television.

It was the kind of progress they would all celebrate because—oh, God, just because they cared. And because that
was what families did. They shared each other's experiences, cheered one another on.

She carefully took another step.

And kept the news to herself.

Every step she took on her own, every walking ability
she recovered, every bit of progress she made, would take
her away from them more quickly. She looked around at
the loved ones she could see, all except Hamish who came
sauntering into the kitchen moments later, and she felt
overwhelmed with the warmth of being part of their family
unit. Yet she felt like an outsider peeking through the window, watching them get on with their lives after she'd
gone.

Hamish smiled at her, unaware, of course, of what she
had just accomplished. She saw his gaze quickly take in
her face—first her eyes, then her nose and mouth and jaw,
and back up to her eyes again.

He stood before her while she stared at the gorgeous,

perfectly formed length of him, from his thick copper hair
to his stocking feet.

"How would you feel about helping with the Christmas
pageant?" he asked abruptly.

"The what?"

He forced a wincing smile as if he dreaded her response.
"Christmas pageant."

"You mean, like manger and Wise Men and 'Joy to the
World'?"

"Pretty much."

"Me?"

"Well," he drawled, half-beseeching, half-wary,
"we're in a bind because Mickey Kostavich's mother had
a stroke and has come to stay with her, so she can't do
the pageant. She's always done it. Tammy volunteered to
take charge, but I know it will be too much for her."

Startled by his request, amused by the irony of a man
like Hamish Chandler being in a pickle because of something as trivial as a church Christmas pageant, B.J. simply
shook her head in disbelief.

She loved this man.

It struck her like a swinging wrecker's ball.

She loved this man with all her heart and soul. She loved
everything about him.

He raised his eyebrows, questioning her response, and
dug his hands into his pockets. She realized then that he
thought she was refusing.

"It means so much to the children. Ours, too," he said
softly.

Ours? Had he said ours? Meaning all the children in his
congregation? Or meaning Emma and Annie, whom he
saw as being the charges of all three adults in the household? She couldn't ask him to clarify. His reference was
at once too thrilling and painful.

"So," she replied, "Emma and Annie participate?"

"Annie finally gets to be an angel this year," he said, his lips twitching into a half smile. "Emma has worked her way up to head shepherd."

"How many children are involved?"

"All who want to be. Maybe about fifty this year."

"Hamish! This is no small thing!"

He smiled at her as though she had just cooed in his ear. "Very true. The New Orleans Mardi Gras pales."

She pressed her eyes shut, her feelings in conflict between frustration and joy. "All right," she told him. "What do you want me to do?"

"Open your eyes, Brenda," he said softly. She did, to find he had moved very close to her, but his hands were still stuffed into his pants pockets. He leaned forward. She was afraid he was going to kiss her and was disappointed when he didn't. "Ask Emma," he said quietly.

"What?"

"Emma will direct you. She knows exactly how they want to look in their costumes. And, of course, call Tammy. I think you'll see all sorts of opportunities to use your talents." He was staring at her with an unnerving intensity, as though what he was saying was less important than whatever it was he was thinking.

"What talents?"

He grinned suggestively. "I think you have many," he said.

Her pulse was racing. She could feel it throbbing in her ears. She couldn't help but know that he wanted her, and although it was exciting beyond words, it saddened her. It was love she wanted to see in his eyes, hear in his voice, sense in his heart. And that was hopeless. She would never measure up to his late wife, or to Tammy Bantz, who was endlessly patient, eternally gentle, as a minister's wife should be.

She lowered her eyes so that he wouldn't see what she

felt for him. She knew they would probably reflect the love and pain and anger that was growing. He would never love her. She would never be acceptable.

"I'll work on your damn pageant," she barked, and pushed him aside as she rose, slid her crutches under her arms and headed for the stairway.

The next day, Hamish wasn't sure Brenda was still speaking to him, not after she went off to bed so angry. If it had been a matter of just getting on her good side, he might have done things differently, or he might even be making an effort right now to relieve her of any responsibility in the pageant.

But the truth was, he needed her help. Tammy Bantz was capable, but between her job, her church responsibilities and her pregnancy, she was spreading herself too thin. And it was impossible to find anyone else less than a month before Christmas. He wasn't sure of all that went into the pageant, but he knew it seemed to take a long time to put together every year.

He couldn't imagine organizing an event with fifty children aged two to ten. Two months ago, he wouldn't have thought Brenda could handle it, either, but he had a different opinion of her now. And he had confidence in her.

Besides, his daughters loved her.

He heard Brenda and the girls in the kitchen, their animated conversation peppered with hooting laughter. He leaned against the wall around the corner for a while and listened. He closed his eyes so that he could visualize Brenda as she looked when she spoke, the sparkling fire in her green eyes, the smile that could have decorated a fashion cover, her soft brown hair bobbing when she swung her head around. She was a beautiful woman.

"Me angel," Annie said, raising her voice over the other two.

"Last year, Michael looked just like a real shepherd," Emma said. Hamish liked the excitement in her voice. "He had on a really cool jacket without sleeves, and it was kind of raggedy on the bottom. And he had on a sweatshirt inside out with a thing tied around his waist."

"Do you suppose you could borrow his costume?" Brenda suggested. Hamish winced, knowing what was coming next.

"Oh, no! No, no, no!" Emma insisted. "I want my own costume. Everybody always makes their own costume."

"I see. What is Michael this year?"

"He gets to be the innkeeper this year. And next year, he'll be a Wise Man, if he's a good boy," she said.

"Me angel," Annie reminded.

"What do angels wear?" Brenda asked.

"Pink!" Annie shouted.

Brenda's soft laugh caught him in the gut. It was a warm laugh, deep and real. He wanted to take her face in his hands and kiss her lips whenever he heard it. "I thought angels always wore white," he heard her say.

"Yeah, they do," Emma agreed.

"Pink!" Annie insisted.

"Will it be all right for her to wear pink?"

Emma didn't answer right away. He could imagine her thinking about it, narrowing her big brown eyes, and then he heard her declare, "I guess so. Everybody makes their own."

"Has anybody ever worn a color? I mean, other than white?"

"I don't think so," Emma said, uncertainty slowing her words.

"Well, I think a blond angel in pale pink will be beautiful," Brenda said. "You might just set a new fashion, Annie."

"Pink angel!" Annie cheered.

"Well, Pink Angel and Ragged Shepherd better finish their cereal so we can get on with the day. The bus will be here soon, Emma," Brenda said.

Hamish took that moment to stride into the kitchen and pour himself a cup of coffee. "Good morning, everyone," he said, eyeing Brenda, watching her reaction.

"Good morning yourself," she said, and he sighed with relief.

When he sat at the table with his cup, their eyes met, and the smile she gave him made him feel armed with enough good feelings to last through the day.

"We're going to go hunting today," she said. "We're going to find whatever we need to create the perfect pink angel costume."

"I never heard of a pink angel," he said to Annie.

"Wow, is your education lacking!" Brenda declared, and Emma giggled.

"And when does the shepherd get costumed?" he asked, pouring dry cereal into a bowl.

"On Saturday, when she isn't in school and we can spend the whole day...hunting," she replied saucily, poking a playful finger into Emma's ribs, inciting another round of giggles.

He poured milk into the bowl. "Hunting? As in shopping?"

"No. Hunting as in...scrounging." She laughed when he raised his eyebrows in doubt. "Anybody can just go *buy* something. The real challenge is in sneaking around, pilfering here and there, going through drawers and closets and boxes. Maybe even the attic, or that little room with all the donated junk in it at the church."

He dropped his spoon. "Donated junk? You mean the poor box?"

"That's a terrible name for it, Hamish. You should call

it, uh, well…'' She stopped a moment to think, then brightened with a dazzling smile. ''Hunter's paradise!''

''But we couldn't take things from the poor people,'' Emma objected quietly.

''It's just called that because every church since medieval times has had a poor box, and it's tradition,'' Hamish said. ''But really, Emma, it's things people don't have any use for anymore, mostly clothes, and it's just like a free garage sale. Anybody can take what they want.''

She nodded in understanding, her big brown eyes narrowed as her busy mind clicked away. He could almost read her every thought, so he wasn't surprised when she turned to Brenda and agreed. ''Then maybe we *should* call it hunter's paradise.''

He tore himself away from them then because there were other things to occupy his mind that day. Edson Forda's supporters were prickling his patience, and he didn't have a sermon for Sunday, and the pile in his In basket was so high it had toppled over onto his desk.

While he worked during the day, he was aware of Brenda and Annie quietly scurrying around the church, talking in hushed voices, opening doors, visiting with the church secretary. At one point, when he was in the hallway, he saw Brenda holding up a length of sheer white curtain while Annie grimaced.

Mrs. Deaton came up behind him. ''That one will tilt your perfect little world a mite, I'd say,'' she predicted sharply, gesturing down the hall toward Brenda's back.

He was about to grin and agree, when the import of her words struck him a sideways blow. Brenda had already caused a few tilts within the congregation. Like the questions about the red sports car parked in his driveway, the fact that she had been to Sunday service only once, and the obvious fact that she no longer needed the Chandlers to take care of her now that she was getting along so well on crutches.

Mostly, though, the tilt was in his own heart, which was full of her.

It was quite incredible, the pain that rocked him when he tried to answer Mrs. Deaton with a short quip. No words came to him, only painful jabs. Brenda had tilted his world all right, and the reason was that she didn't belong there.

He'd been forgetting that too often lately. When they were at home like a close and loving family, he found himself struggling furiously not to take her in his arms and lay her down to love her as thoroughly and passionately as he could imagine. Or when she and the girls and Mrs. B were laughing or playing or cooking or disagreeing. Or fomenting some playful plotting.

Brenda was good at that. Tilting something off its rusty axis. Generally, he enjoyed watching her do it. And generally, whatever it was *needed* some tilting, he thought. She had a refreshing way of looking at things, a courageous nature and an independent spirit.

He was finding anguish too often overwhelming his joy because the joy was as temporary as she was. His was not a life for her. His was not a life she could ever want or adjust to. It was obvious now even though she was visibly enjoying her activity with Annie, wrapped up as they were in a common cause.

Suddenly, Mrs. Deaton gripped his wrist, startling him, and he turned abruptly to study her face.

He saw understanding there so profound it embarrassed him.

She gave him a squeeze and barked, "I'll see you in your office about this committee business." Then she strode briskly ahead to wait for him there.

He wondered if his feelings for Brenda were leaving messages on his face. It was a frightening thought.

Chapter Ten

B.J. was immediately absorbed into the pageant effort, first because it was so very important to Emma and Annie, then because she was having fun with it and then because Hamish—always hovering nearby, it seemed—was so supportive and grateful and, apparently, even impressed.

Besides, she was needed.

Tammy's doctor had advised her to slow down, so B.J. found herself spreading her wings over the entire project for the time being. Mickey Kostavich was still involved in an advisory capacity and had made arrangements for her mother's care to enable her to take over full-time the last five days before Christmas Eve.

B.J. found that her suggestions were usually a little too nontraditional for Mickey, but then, she was the first to admit that as much as she enjoyed what she was doing, she was only masquerading in the role.

She thought there ought to be more candles and fewer electric lights in the decorations. And she thought they ought to use real evergreen boughs and some of the early

American decorating ideas people had used before there were modern utilities and shopping malls.

B.J. didn't like the cold, fake appearance of the cheap little doll that was supposed to play the Baby Jesus in the manger. So she took it upon herself to find a more realistic, softer-looking baby mannequin.

She and Annie had disagreed at first about her costume, but once they'd dyed the sheer white and lace curtains a pale pink and cut them into pattern pieces, Annie was ecstatic. B.J. didn't tell Tammy that Annie was going to be a pink angel and she persuaded both sisters that it would be a nice surprise during the pageant if they could keep it a secret. Just in case it caused a negative reaction prematurely.

And one Saturday, the decorating committee showed up, and she had to get acquainted with a large group of men and women of all ages, including some teens, who began spreading all the old and newly purchased decorations over the floor of the narthex and nave and setting the stage.

So this was the Christmas spirit, B.J. thought in wonder. Hot punch suddenly appeared, and sandwiches, lovely ones, filled with ham salad and smoked turkey and Italian salami. And people who had been disagreeing became remarkably agreeable, even joyful, laughing and eating, joking about a crooked wreath or a dangling light string, congratulating and ridiculing in easy camaraderie.

Being a newcomer to the pageant, she held her tongue when she thought she had a better idea and merely observed. Just when she wished Hamish would turn up to see what fun everyone was having and how festive his church was becoming, he did appear. He accepted half a sandwich and a cup of punch and praised them in detail, wandering around and looking up as if he had never seen the church decorated before.

Later that night, she challenged him on his playacting.

"I can tell, Hamish, they use just about the same decorations every year, and you've been the pastor here for...how long? Six, seven years? So it's the same every year, and you walked around and oohed and aahed as if you'd never seen them before."

Anyone else would have been insulted, but then, he was uniquely Hamish. True to form, he answered her as if he had been eager for her question. "Every year, it seems to be done a little differently, I think, because every time I see the decorations going up, it's like the first time. I love the Christmas decorations. I love the season. I like what it does for people. I wish everyone could feel what I do. I'm very grateful for all of this."

His words nearly brought tears to her eyes, not only because of his boyish sincerity, but because she loved him so much and wanted to hold him, and she couldn't.

"It's a shame," she told Hamish at dinner one night, "there are so many nice things in the poor box, and I think people are too proud to even be seen looking through them. No one really seems to be taking advantage of it."

He had been distracted since coming home, she noted, and reacted with uncharacteristic impatience. "What would you suggest?"

"A sale."

"You mean, charge people for what's there to be given to them free?"

"Yes. Definitely." Her patience was being tested, too, because he seemed much too thickheaded tonight. "It's no damage to one's pride to shop for bargains," she argued, although that was something she had learned just recently. "Everybody loves a bargain, even the wealthy. We could set prices really low and let people haggle them down even further. The pile of stuff in there is really big, Hamish."

"And it wouldn't be obvious? Our intention to help the

poor while saving their pride?'' He looked at her pointedly. ''That sounds to me about as effective as changing the name of 'charity' to 'welfare' so people don't feel bad about getting it.''

He had her there, she had to admit. During the evening, she thought about it some more.

''What if we called it a fund-raiser?'' she asked later, interrupting him as he worked at his desk in the study.

He leaned back in his chair, his formerly grim expression softened to one of weariness. He rubbed a hand over his face as he replied, ''Maybe. Go on.''

She sat by his desk, her heart lurching because she wanted to soothe away the fatigue lines around his eyes and mouth. ''We could say we're raising money for some fancy lights for the outside Christmas tree. We could do it after services on Sunday. The outside tree-lighting ceremony is Thursday.''

He studied her for a few moments, the fatigue achingly visible in his handsome face. It took willpower not to reach out to him.

''I think it's a good idea, Brenda,'' he said. ''If you can pull it off. I'm afraid I can't give you any help.''

''What is it, Hamish?'' she queried, her hand reaching out to stroke his shoulder. She hadn't meant to do that. ''You're exhausted.''

''I love this season, but there are things that get me down,'' he explained, looking into her eyes, sending a charge through her body. ''Would you believe this is the worst time of year for family crises? And it's a very lonely time of year for people who have no one or nowhere to go.''

She hadn't thought of that, but she knew it was true. Hadn't she been one of those people for most of her life?

She had spent the past several Christmases working because there simply was nothing else as interesting to do.

Before that, she had partied with other singles, once at a ski lodge, another time at a golf club, sometimes at someone's house or condo somewhere.

Christmas had never before been a special time for her.

She rose and moved around to his back and slowly rubbed his neck. He stiffened at first, then relaxed as she hoped he would, and his head fell forward. She looked at the back of his loose-knit sweater, at the slightly fraying collar of his shirt, at his thick, coarse hair the color of dark copper. She felt the iron of his muscles under her fingers and the solid, square shape of his large shoulders.

She fought an intense urge to pull up the sweater and pull down the shirt and put her lips against his shoulder and his neck. She wanted to run her fingers through his beautiful shaggy hair and breathe deeply the scent of him. It was difficult to hold back. It was very difficult, almost impossible.

She stopped, tightened her grip on his neck and leaned down, rubbing her cheek against his, whispering, "Go to bed, Hamish. Get some sleep." Then she abruptly removed her hands and fled.

The aching was intense, choking her. She slipped quickly by Mrs. B and the girls watching TV and hid in her room, where rare tears were her release.

During the next week, B.J. kept busy and added to her own self-appointed responsibilities by taking her camera along. Her motivation was twofold. Consciously, she wanted to garner and preserve as many memories as possible. Then there was that other reason she could never define. She took pictures because she somehow felt a compulsion from deep in her soul to do so.

She called Tammy Bantz to find out how one went about organizing a fund-raising sale, and Tammy replied, "Oh, but I wouldn't know about that. I never get involved, unless they need an extra hand.''

"Why ever not?" B.J. asked.

"A pastor's wife has to be very careful not to throw her weight around," she said. "People would be very critical of that.''

B.J. felt oddly deflated, as if Tammy's words had been a personal criticism. But then, it was just another confirmation of her unsuitability to be Hamish's mate. After all, hadn't Tammy's mentor been Hamish's wife? Don't even *think* about that, she warned herself. There was already too much hurt involved in her situation.

She ended up simply doing it her way, with a little advice from Mickey and, of all people, the forbidding Mrs. Deaton. She made sale notices and ran them off on Hamish's office copier, using bright purple paper, which caused the secretary to shake her head in disapproval.

B.J. continued to work on the pageant, taking pictures every day and some evenings. On Wednesday night, she played volleyball, sort of, using one crutch, hobbling, eliciting guffaws and good-natured wisecracks. She didn't last long, but she had at least given it a try and even perspired a little. Hamish had always been close by, she knew, ready to catch her if she fell and silently encouraging her with his heart-stopping smile.

She saw him frequently during the day, even though he was busier than usual, and they were almost always together with the girls and Mrs. B in the evening.

On Saturday, twelve days before Christmas, the five of them decorated the tree in the living room, a misshapen tree with a crooked trunk donated by a member of his congregation. "We'll make it beautiful," B.J. said to the little girls, who looked at it as if it were ruined pie. "Think we can? Are we good enough? Let's do it!" She clapped her hands to convey enthusiasm, and eventually they began to feel better about it. They literally buried the little pine needles in decorations, then laughed at how festive and overdressed it looked.

She caught Hamish's eye when they were done. He was holding Annie up to place a little white angel on the top. His gaze was intense. Unnerving.

"Next year, we'll color it pink," she said playfully, then looked quickly away. She had spoken without thinking. Next year, she would be history in this family. Maybe a real Mrs. Chandler would be decorating the tree with them.

Thinking about the future sobered her. She sank onto the lumpy couch and committed the overdecorated tree to memory. Hamish set Annie down, and she came to B.J., putting a soft, chubby arm around her neck. "Don't be sad. Is boo'ful," she said.

"So are you," B.J. whispered, and buried her face for a moment in the child's fine, long blond hair, then adjusted the pretty pink-and-mauve bows above her ear.

Sunday was the sale, which was a success. Nearly everything was gone by the time it was over at two in the afternoon. What remained was returned to the poor box.

The money from the fund-raiser bought some flashing lights for the outside tree, so that the annual ceremony on Thursday night was something special and attracted a larger crowd than usual. B.J. and Hamish and the girls huddled together in heavy coats to participate. Afterward, people sang carols and drank hot chocolate, and some of the young ones got in a snowball fight.

When there was a week until Christmas, B.J. took her negatives to the newspaper for printing. Her prints turned out as beautiful as the people in them, she thought, and she decided to make a memory book of photos for the Chandlers as a Christmas gift.

On the Saturday before Christmas, B.J. officially

stepped down as pageant coordinator and gave Mickey the reins, then she fled from the room, stricken and sad.

In the doorway, she encountered a latecomer. "Well, Brenda," the woman said, "you've recuperated nicely, haven't you? Still living with the pastor?"

B.J. mumbled what she hoped was a diplomatic reply, then hurried to her car. During the short ride home, she began to tremble, finally admitting to herself how obvious it must be to everyone else that she was well enough to take care of herself.

She had hoped to postpone the inevitable until after Christmas, telling herself it was because of the girls, because it would upset them and make their Christmas less happy. But that was a lie. She wanted to procrastinate. She wanted to delay her heartbreak for as long as possible.

When she turned off the engine in Hamish's driveway, she resolved to do what she knew she should have done weeks ago.

That night, after Mrs. B and Annie had gone to bed and while Emma was watching a Christmas special on TV, B.J. invaded Hamish's study. "We have to talk," she said.

As if he knew what she had in mind, he hesitated for just the precise moment to make his question pointed. "Is it really necessary?"

"I think it is," she replied quickly, sitting in the chair by his desk.

He pushed his seat back, but his movements were sluggish, and he was oddly quiet. He rose and strode slowly in a circle within the small room. She noticed a slump to his back, which she assumed was because he was very tired.

"Are you all right?" she asked.

When he turned to her, she was shocked to see his face looking ravaged, his eyes tight with raw pain. "You're leaving," he rasped.

The two words sent waves of anguish through her very soul. How could she bear it? To leave him. To leave the girls who had become as close to her as if they were her own?

"Before Christmas?" he challenged. "What do you think that will do to Emma and Annie? They love you. They think of you as part of the family."

She understood his concern for his daughters and wished instead that he had wanted her to stay because... But that was a foolish fantasy.

"I'll be back on Christmas Day," she said as her heart was shattering.

"Brenda's leaving? Why? Did we do something bad?" Emma's voice from the doorway startled them. She was clutching the door frame as if it might tumble apart without her support.

"No, sweetheart, nobody did anything bad," Hamish said slowly, his voice low. "She has her own home to go back to, and a job, and friends."

"But this is her home, and we're her family," Emma protested, eyes glistening. B.J. heard the dry sob that followed her words and saw a tear slide down Emma's cheek. "Don't you love us anymore, Brenda?"

She felt her own eyes stinging at the thought of leaving Emma behind. "Of course I still love you. I love all of you. Very, very much. But this has been my home only for a while. Your daddy let me come here until I got well, and I'm well now. In fact, honey, I've been well for a long time. But...I didn't want to leave. I like it here."

"You can stay. Can't she, Daddy? You can stay. We don't want you to go, and you don't want to leave. Why can't you just stay?"

If she replied, she would cry, so B.J. flew up from the chair and turned her back on them.

"Yes," Hamish said softly from behind her, moving

himself gently against her, pressing the full length of his warm, large body to her back, curling his fingers around her shoulders. "Why can't you just stay?"

B.J. closed her eyes and leaned into him. She felt his hands come around and fold over her upper chest under her chin. She laid her head back on his shoulder and fought to keep her tears at bay.

"Daddy wants you to stay, too, Brenda. Why can't you stay? I can tell you like us. I can tell you like Daddy especially. Why can't you stay?"

B.J. slowly, deliberately, uncrossed his arms and pulled his hands down to the sides, then shuffled away from him. She took several careful, sliding steps forward, keeping her back to both of them. "You're making this very difficult. You're making me the heavy," she choked.

"What's a heavy, Daddy?" Emma quizzed.

"I think Brenda and I better talk about this," Hamish told his daughter. "If you want to watch TV for a while, I'll come in and take you to bed when we're done."

"You talk her into staying, Daddy," Emma said in her usual sunny way, as if giving him an assignment she had no doubt he could achieve. She kissed him on the cheek and then skipped away. He quietly shut the door behind her and turned to Brenda, who felt ravaged by the circumstances.

"Why now?" he demanded. "Why now, Brenda?"

Hamish was frantic to change her mind, to make her see she needed him and the girls. But she had given him no indication that she loved him as anything more than a close friend. Over the past few weeks, he had touched her, embraced her, shown her that he wanted her in every appropriate way he knew, and she had not responded.

Usually she stiffened or pulled away, obviously repulsed.

Trying to keep her in his home wasn't going to attract

her. Keeping her close wasn't going to change her feelings for him. He knew that. And hated the thought. Furthermore, it was selfish to hold her here when she was ready to leave, when she wanted to get on with her life. Oh, it was plain enough that she had found a refuge in his house and that she had accepted his family as her own, but she had not accepted him in the way he wanted her to.

He didn't want to believe it had all just been an interesting diversion for her. It hurt to think that.

He had demanded to know why her timing was so bad, in effect accusing her of being insensitive to the girls. That had been unfair of him, he knew.

"I'm sorry," he said. "You have every right to leave whenever you think it's right for you."

"I probably should have waited until after Christmas. I just thought..." Her voice trailed off. He could see she had no intention of finishing the sentence.

"When?" he asked, sinking heavily into the chair behind his desk.

"In the morning. Very early. Before anyone is up."

He cleared his throat and looked at her directly. "It's so sudden. For the girls."

She winced and looked down at her feet. "I know, but it isn't going to be easy no matter how or when I do it, is it? I mean, I'm going to miss them just as much no matter when I...go."

He could see she was genuine in the loss she was feeling. She and his daughters had come to love each other deeply. "I'll talk to them," he said. "I'll try to help them understand. Anyway, you'll just be gone a few days and then be back on Christmas Day. You will spend the day with us?"

She nodded a little wildly. He could see she was too emotional to speak.

"All right. I'll tell the girls and Mrs. Billings," he

agreed, putting more self-assurance into his voice than he felt. Frankly, he wanted to put his head down on the desk and weep. She was crushing the life out of him, leaving him mortally wounded.

She took a few shuffling steps to the wall where she had leaned her crutch and in one agile movement, she placed it under her arm, so different from her clumsy ways in the past.

Then she was gone.

He laid his head down on his desk, but fought succumbing to the pain. He would have to be strong to explain things to his daughters tomorrow. They would be brokenhearted. Not as brokenhearted as he, but brokenhearted nonetheless.

When he found Emma half-asleep in the living room, he lifted her in his arms and carried her upstairs. "We better not tell Annie tonight," she mumbled. "She might not be able to sleep."

He hugged her close and tightly, his brave little daughter, and silently apologized for failing to attract the stepmother he wanted for her.

It was depressing to step into her condo, which had a foreign smell, a chilled feeling of bleak dormancy, as though it no longer belonged to her. It certainly didn't feel like hers, but more like a forgotten place from a life she had abandoned.

B.J. checked her watch and saw that the Chandlers were likely arriving home after Sunday service. She thought about the people she had come to know and like, people who had accepted her, people she knew she should have said farewell to.

She regretted that she could not bring herself to leave the girls while they were awake. Instead, she had slipped silently into their bedroom and kissed them while they slept. Nothing in the fiercely independent life she had led had prepared her for the ragged pain of saying goodbye to people she loved.

She called her father, who typically liked to sleep off his Sunday-morning hangovers, and left a brief message on his machine.

She called the photo editor at home that afternoon and discovered she would need a physician's release in order to return to work officially. She could freelance as an independent, but to get back on the regular payroll, she would need the release.

Monday morning, she called Dr. Wahler for an appointment and bullied his nurse into working her in on Wednesday.

She shopped for a few groceries, then wandered through the holiday-decorated Minneapolis skyways to buy last-minute gifts for the Chandlers and Mrs. B, forcing herself not to go overboard on Hamish, who needed so many things.

Everywhere she went, Hamish was with her, his voice, his smile. His touch. She saw him in countless heavy-knit sweaters and chinos, in tailored blazers and tight jeans. What a pleasure it would be to buy for him and to run her hands over the fabrics when he tried them on for the first time.

Would she ever get over him? Would she ever manage to let an hour go by when she didn't think about him?

She went through the motions of ordering her father's offbeat Christmas present from Neiman Marcus. It was a tradition with them to order something useless and expensive for each other in a typically macho spoof of the holiday. Her heart certainly wasn't in it this year, and the tradition suddenly seemed false and sophomoric.

She looked at the telephone countless times, and each

time the choking in her throat told her she would have a devil of a time staying away from Hamish.

She ate a solitary TV dinner, half of which she threw out because she couldn't swallow it. If she had stayed, if she were part of the family for real, she'd have been sitting across the table from him, with Annie and Mrs. Billings on her left and Emma on her right.

Her eyes were drawn frequently to the bare wall where Hamish had removed the framed photos that still hung in his bedroom. Would he think of her when he looked at them? Would he only think of her as that crippled woman, that photographer, a nice friend for his daughters?

On Wednesday, she met with Dr. Wahler and asked for the release to return to work. He authorized her to return part-time and made arrangements for her to attend a rehab center near the newspaper office for her continued therapy. He also gave her a thumbs-up on using a cane. But for some reason, none of this made her happy.

On Christmas Eve she sat alone, staring at her uneaten dinner, not sorry she had turned down an invitation from her editor. She thought of the pageant about to start at eight, and the Midnight Service, which actually began at ten.

She couldn't bear it, not seeing the pageant. They wouldn't have to know she was there. She could slip in late, sit in the back.

She had to be there.

She had to do it. Driving to Kolstad, she thought of going through life without Hamish's solid strength behind her. She thought of the years ahead, of being his friend, of visiting him and being hugged and having her hand held when she needed him. And she thought of coming to the house one day to meet a strange woman he would introduce as his new bride.

It was too much. It just hurt too damned much. Like dull knife blades tearing through flesh. Worse. Much worse even than that.

She parked a long way from the church and used her new cane to help her get there. The pageant was just beginning when she slipped by the poor-box door and noted the new hand-lettered Hunter's Paradise sign. Something caught in her throat at the gesture.

She slid into a small space at the end of the last row in the all-purpose room and watched the pageant. She couldn't hold back the tears when she saw the pale pink of the littlest angel flitting across the stage. Or when the head shepherd spoke her lines loud and clear. Or when the pastor, standing against the wall near the front, applauded with contagious enthusiasm at the end. She watched as Mrs. B herded the girls to the coatracks, knowing the housekeeper was taking them home for a good night's sleep. Then she walked to her car and sat behind the wheel. She started it eventually so that she could run the heater, but she couldn't bring herself to drive away.

At ten o'clock, she returned to the church, made her way up the stairs to the back of the choir loft and participated in Hamish's beautiful Christmas Eve service. She wept through most of it, even while she sang the carols, then forcing herself to stop, she dried her eyes before it was over.

The people had all gone when she made her way down. She knew Hamish would still be there. Her actions were now beyond her control. Something else was driving her. She found herself making her way to the little room off the altar, the room where he dressed and stored his vestments and extra prayer books.

She found him standing at a narrow window, looking out at flecks of snow silently wandering out of the sky under the lights in the parking lot. He stood very still and

alone, surrounded by silence. He stood tall and strong, her
Hamish.

"Hello," she said.

"Come in, Brenda." His voice was gentle. He turned
slowly to face her. "I knew you were there."

"You were waiting for me?"

He nodded. She didn't like the weariness in his face.
She was determined not to cry, but it was difficult. Too
difficult, she realized.

"I can't stay," she cried, frantic to be out of his sight
before she turned into a gusher.

"Not yet. I have things to say to you," he said softly.
"Please, sit down."

"Tomorrow," she replied in desperation. "I have to go
now." She felt her insides clench like a fighting fist. Any
moment, she was going to start weeping.

"Not yet," he said, stepping closer, grasping her arms
above the elbows. "I've been thinking about this since you
left. I was hoping to speak to you privately before tomorrow. There are things that need to be said. We need to
clear the air, to get things out into the open. Between us."

"No," she gasped, burying her face in her hands. "I
don't want to hear. I know I'm not marriage material,
Hamish. I don't know what's so bad about me, but I accept
that...I accept our friendship and I just can't...listen to
you tell me—"

"Brenda."

She couldn't bear to hear more, but he continued anyway.

"You're the only one who thinks you're not marriage
material," he said.

"I...what?"

"You're excellent marriage material," he assured her
warmly. "You're brave and loving. You're creative and
honest. You've done wonders for Annie and you've given

both girls something they haven't had in a long, long time.'' She saw him wince as he added, "I know you could never settle down in a little town, to a humdrum life…'' He paused for a moment, then spoke softly. "You're trembling. I don't want you to be afraid.''

"I don't want to hear,'' she wailed.

"Your worst fears have probably come true,'' he persisted with a small smile of irony. "I have found myself very strongly attracted to you.''

He loosened his grasp and slid his arms up and then down around her elbows. She could see that he was fighting with himself, that what he was saying was not easy for him.

"What I want you to know is that I love you very much, Brenda Jane, with my whole heart and soul. I love you the way a man loves a woman he wants to spend the rest of his life with. I won't embarrass you by asking formally, but I want you to know that if you returned my feelings, if you had by some miracle managed to fall in love with me, I would want you to be my wife.''

Silence.

There was only silence as her mind whirled and her heart seemed to stop and start and stop again.

He grimaced, then continued, "You are marriage material, Brenda Jane, and more than that.'' His eyes studied her face, roaming over her hair, cheeks, mouth, focusing at last on her eyes. "You're beautiful and you're a natural mother.''

She watched his throat jump as he swallowed hard. His hands slid up to cup her jaw.

"You're the woman I want to be the mother of my children,'' he whispered. "Not only of Annie and Emma, but the ones yet to be born.''

She saw the pain in his eyes when she only stared and didn't reply.

"I can see how much this might embarrass you, but I had to say it," he said huskily. "I had hoped..."

She opened her mouth to make a response, but only a sob escaped, and tears spilled over her cheeks.

"Don't cry," he whispered. "I'm not asking anything of you. And I wouldn't hurt you for the world."

She shook her head from side to side in an effort to communicate, then finally shook his hands off and threw herself against him, clutching at the back of his shirt, kissing wildly at the fabric in front. "Hamish, Hamish," she cried. "Oh, Hamish."

His arms came around her tentatively. She understood his confusion. All her life she'd been the smart mouth, quick on the uptake, ready with an insult. And now, at the most momentous instant of her life, she couldn't seem to express a coherent thought.

"Brenda?"

She gripped him tighter.

"Say something," he whispered in desperation.

She looked up at him. "Are my pictures still hanging in your bedroom?"

He paused, then answered warily, "They're the last thing I see before sleep and the first thing when I wake. I hope you don't want them back."

"Oh, but I do. I, too, became accustomed to seeing them morning and night, and I'd like to continue that."

"Then you'll have to give me something else," he said, nuzzling her neck.

"I intend to, Hamish. I intend to give you what I've wanted to give you for a long, long time." She pulled away to look up at him in awe, clasping the sides of his shirt in her fists. He was going to get more than he bargained for. He was going to find out that she had been intended for him all along.

Only for him. It would be her gift to him on their wedding night.

"I don't understand...."

"I've never been in love before, so I don't know exactly how to do this, but I'd like to apply for the position you have open here, the one you said you'd ask me to take if I was interested." She laughed in utter and complete jubilation. "I've discovered it doesn't matter if I'm not qualified."

He grinned and held her close, enfolding her very tightly in his arms. "Ah, dear lady. And here I was afraid you were overqualified." Then he whispered in her ear, "Merry, Merry Christmas."

"My name is Brenda Jane," she whispered back against his chest. "And Merry Christmas yourself."

*   *   *   *   *

CHRISTINE FLYNN

Continues the twelve-book series—36 HOURS—in December 1997 with Book Six

FATHER AND CHILD REUNION

Eve Stuart was back, and Rio Redtree couldn't ignore the fact that her daughter bore his Native American features. So, Eve had broken his heart *and* kept him from his child! But this was no time for grudges, because his little girl and her mother, the woman he had never stopped—could never stop—loving, were in danger, and Rio would stop at nothing to protect *his* family.

For Rio and Eve and *all* the residents of Grand Springs, Colorado, the storm-induced blackout was just the beginning of 36 Hours that changed *everything*! You won't want to miss a single book.

Available at your favorite retail outlet.

Look us up on-line at: http://www.romance.net

36HRS6

Welcome to the Towers!

In January
New York Times bestselling author

NORA ROBERTS

takes us to the fabulous Maine coast mansion
haunted by a generations-old secret and introduces
us to the fascinating family that lives there.

Mechanic Catherine "C.C." Calhoun and hotel magnate
Trenton St. James mix like axle grease and mineral
water—until they kiss. Efficient Amanda Calhoun finds
easygoing Sloan O'Riley insufferable—and irresistible.
And they all must race to solve the mystery
surrounding a priceless hidden emerald necklace.

Catherine and Amanda

THE Calhoun Women

**A special 2-in-1 edition containing
COURTING CATHERINE and A MAN FOR AMANDA.**

Look for the next installment of
THE CALHOUN WOMEN with Lilah and Suzanna's
stories, coming in March 1998.

Available at your favorite retail outlet.

Silhouette®

As seen on TV!
Free Gift Offer

With a Free Gift proof-of-purchase from any Silhouette® book,
you can receive a beautiful cubic zirconia pendant.

This gorgeous marquise-shaped stone is a genuine cubic
zirconia—accented by an 18" gold tone necklace.
(Approximate retail value $19.95)

Send for yours today...
compliments of *Silhouette*®
™

To receive your free gift, a cubic zirconia pendant, send us one original proof-of-
purchase, photocopies not accepted, from the back of any Silhouette Romance™,
Silhouette Desire®, Silhouette Special Edition®, Silhouette Intimate Moments®
or Silhouette Yours Truly™ title available at your favorite retail outlet, together with
the Free Gift Certificate, plus a check or money order for $1.65 U.S./$2.15 CAN. (do
not send cash) to cover postage and handling, payable to Silhouette Free Gift Offer.
We will send you the specified gift. Allow 6 to 8 weeks for delivery. Offer good until
December 31, 1997, or while quantities last. Offer valid in the U.S. and Canada only.

Free Gift Certificate

Name: _____

Address: _____

City: _____ State/Province: _____ Zip/Postal Code: _____

Mail this certificate, one proof-of-purchase and a check or money order for postage
and handling to: SILHOUETTE FREE GIFT OFFER 1997. In the U.S.: 3010 Walden
Avenue, P.O. Box 9077, Buffalo NY 14269-9077. In Canada: P.O. Box 613, Fort Erie,
Ontario L2Z 5X3.

FREE GIFT OFFER   084-KFD
ONE PROOF-OF-PURCHASE
To collect your fabulous FREE GIFT, a cubic zirconia pendant, you must include this
original proof-of-purchase for each gift with the properly completed Free Gift Certificate.

084-KFDR

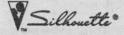